Sadie Rose
AND THE SECRET ROMANCE

A SADIE ROSE ADVENTURE

Sadie Rose
AND THE
SECRET ROMANCE

Hilda Stahl

CROSSWAY BOOKS • WHEATON, ILLINOIS
A DIVISION OF GOOD NEWS PUBLISHERS

Sadie Rose and the Secret Romance.

Copyright © 1992 by Wordspinners, Inc.

Published by Crossway Books, a division of Good News Publishers, 1300 Crescent Street, Wheaton, Illinois 60187.

Cover illustration: Kathy Kulin

First printing, 1992

Printed in the United States of America

ISBN 0-89107-661-1

00		99		98		97		96		95		94		93		92
15	14	13	12	11	10	9	8	7	6	5	4	3	2	1

*Dedicated with love
to Andrea Boyer*

Contents

A Race After Babe

Her patched and faded dress pressing tightly around her thin legs, Sadie raced across the vast Nebraska prairie to head off their calf Babe. Dew-wet grass soaked and chilled her bare feet. The wind caught at her bonnet and tore it off her head. It dangled down her back as her long brown braids danced across her thin shoulders. She widened the circle between her and Babe so she could cut her off. She didn't want Babe running farther into the sandhills where she would be torn apart by wild cats or coyotes. Babe had pushed her way out when Sadie had turned Bossie into the corral after milking her. Babe liked her freedom.

"Tanner!" Sadie shouted. The chilly October wind ripped the word from her mouth and flung it toward the sod house where Momma, Opal, Helen, and Web were already preparing dinner for the company they were expecting later. "Tanner!" Sadie shouted again. Then she remembered Tanner had gone to the west pasture with Caleb and Riley. Sadie bit back a groan. If Tanner had been home he'd be after Babe in a flash to herd her back to the corral. Tanner belonged to the whole family, but in her heart Sadie knew he was really only hers. She'd saved his life when he was just a pup. Now he obeyed every command she gave him.

Sadie ran faster, her bare feet barely touching the dew-wet grass. She didn't have time to chase Babe this morning. It was almost time to get ready for Sunday meeting. Since they'd moved to the edge of the sandhills to live on the Circle Y Ranch with Caleb York as their new pa, they'd had Sunday meeting at their house. Church in Jake's Crossing was too far away to attend. Weather permitting, neighbors gathered every Sunday at the Circle Y for singing and Bible study. Today she'd see her best friend Mary. And she'd see Levi Cass! Her pulse leaped and she almost lost stride. Levi had turned seventeen in August and she was close to thirteen. Maybe by the time she was fifteen he'd look at her the way he had once looked at Cousin Gerda. With Gerda soon to marry Gabe Hepford, Levi just might start making eyes at Opal again. And that wouldn't do at all!

Sadie turned Babe slightly, but not enough to head her back to the corral. Instead she ran around a low hill out of sight of the ranch buildings. A pain stabbed Sadie's side and her lungs burned, but she kept running. Momma would tan her hide good and maybe Caleb would too if she let Babe get away.

Flynn Greer reined his palomino closer to the wagon Barr Eldred was driving. "What's that up ahead?" Flynn called, pointing with his gloved hand.

Barr narrowed his brown eyes. "Looks like a girl trying to catch a cow." He didn't much care what was out there. He was way past being hungry. He was close to starving.

"She runs like the wind," Flynn replied thoughtfully. He was always on the lookout for a way to bring in cash. If he could take the girl, run her in races, and take bets, he just might make enough to tide him over for the coming winter. This winter Barr would have to fend for himself. Flynn glanced at Barr and frowned. He wasn't really worth his salt now that he was thirteen and growing again. When he was a little shaver folks took to him. They thought he was a fine man for taking on an orphan, especially such a scruffy one, with him being so young himself. It had paid off well. Barr could con folks with the best of them.

Flynn lifted the rope off his saddle horn. He'd give the girl a hand, get her to trust him, then ride off with her before she knew what was happening to her. "I'll be back directly," he said, nudging Kit.

Barr sighed heavily. They'd been up since dawn and still hadn't taken time for breakfast and a warm fire. He was hungry and cold and tired of the endless sandhills.

Easing out the loop, Flynn urged Kit to a gallop. He swung the loop wide and when he was close enough to the young heifer he let it fly. It settled as pretty as you please around the heifer's neck. He still hadn't lost his touch, even after all the years of being away from ranch life. Abruptly he pushed the thought aside. He wouldn't let himself remember anything concerning the ranch or his family. On his

11

own Kit stopped, jerking the heifer off her feet. Flynn patted Kit's neck and grinned.

Sadie had seen the man riding toward Babe with his loop out. She slowed to a stop several feet away and her chest rose and fell. The man was good looking and had a friendly smile. "Thanks, mister," she said breathlessly. "I thought I might have to give up and get my pa."

Flynn shot a look around, but didn't see anyone else. Maybe he'd have to change his plans. "Is your pa close by?"

Sadie nodded. She watched the boy on the covered wagon stop the team beside the man on the palomino. The boy looked cold and unhappy. He was about her age and as whipcord thin as Web. The team rattled the harness and moved restlessly. The boy settled them with a soft word. Sadie turned back to the man. "The Circle Y is around that hill. You're welcome to stop in and water your horses and have breakfast. If you care to, you can stay for Sunday meeting."

His interest immediately sparked, Flynn pushed his hat to the back of his head. His dark hair curled over his ears and sprang to life where his hat had been. His blue eyes flashed with interest. "And what's Sunday meeting?"

"The neighbors get together for hymn singing and Bible reading," Sadie said, as she pushed a wisp of dark hair off her flushed cheek.

Flynn wasn't much interested in hymns or the Bible even though he'd grown up with both, but the people attending were of great interest.

Sadie flipped her braids back over her thin shoulders. "We don't have a church closer than Jake's Crossing, so we make do."

Flynn took off his hat and bowed toward Sadie.

He'd almost given up finding people in the sandhills he could sell his wares to. What better folks than good Christians? His idea of taking Sadie left his mind as he thought about selling cast-iron stoves, windmills, and barbed wire fencing. "Me and Barr would be pleased to join you and your neighbors. I play guitar and would be glad to join in with the singing."

"Caleb York plays guitar too," Sadie announced proudly. "He's my daddy." After Pa died in the blizzard and Momma married Caleb, it had taken Sadie a while to learn to love him and to call him Daddy. But now it was second nature.

"You climb right up on the wagon while I tie your heifer to the back," Flynn said as he nudged Kit forward. He stopped and doffed his hat with a grin. "I reckon I better introduce myself and this boy here. I'm Flynn Greer and this is Barr Eldred. I'm a salesman and Barr helps me in any way he can."

Barr nodded, but didn't smile.

Sadie smiled and said, "Howdy."

Barr's stomach grumbled with hunger as he watched Flynn. He could tell Flynn was up to no good again, but he didn't much care what Flynn had in mind as long as he could fill his empty stomach and get warm.

Sadie climbed up on the high seat and sat beside Barr. She wondered why he didn't smile, then figured he was shy. His lips were blue and he shivered. "Cold mornin'," she declared.

"Real cold." He moved so Sadie wasn't touching him.

Flynn climbed to the high seat, pushing Barr off. "You ride Kit so I can talk to Sadie."

Barr did as he was told. He always did what he

13

was told. He'd learned that long ago after his folks died in a fire and he was left on the streets to fend for himself.

Sadie retied her old brown bonnet and rubbed her hands over her knees to smoothe down the patched calico dress. Her feet were dirty and she hoped Flynn or Barr hadn't noticed they were bare. When she changed into her Sunday dress she'd also have to put on shoes. Caleb had bought new shoes for her last month in Jake's Crossing. They were too big, but she knew she'd grow into them now that she'd finally started growing again. Momma had said she probably always would be small for her age since she took after Grandma.

"You come from a big family?" Flynn asked as he urged the black mares forward.

Sadie braced her feet to keep from falling against Flynn as the wagon bounced along the uneven prairie. "There are five of us kids and Momma and Daddy. Daddy was an orphan from Texas. He brought cattle from Texas to graze here and decided he wanted his own place. Momma's from Michigan and she talks all the time about tree-covered land. She loves trees."

Flynn laughed. He liked listening to Sadie.

Sadie folded her hands primly in her lap. "Riley's sixteen, soon to be seventeen. He never took to being a farmer, but he loves ranchin'. Then there's Opal. She's fifteen and wishes she was sixteen so she could get married." Sadie shrugged. "Then there's me. I'll be thirteen come December. Webster just turned ten and Helen is nine." Sadie smiled at the man and he smiled back. Opal would be excited about seeing him. He was probably too old for her, but Opal wouldn't care. She was always on the look-out for a fine young man. And Flynn

14

was a handsome man with a lot of charm. "You got a family?"

Flynn's stomach cramped, but he kept a smile on his face. He didn't like thinking about his family.

Sadie saw the pain in his eyes and felt sorry she'd asked.

"Barr and me stick together. We're close to family, I reckon."

Barr urged Kit to a faster walk. He didn't want to hear Flynn tell about him.

"I found him a few years back wandering the streets in some town I don't recollect the name of back when I first started selling."

"Sioux City," Barr commented over his shoulder. Flynn might as well get it right if he was bound to tell it.

Flynn nodded. "Yup. Sioux City, Iowa. You ever been there, Sadie York?"

She shook her head. "But we lived in Douglas County near Omaha before we moved here."

"You're a long way from Douglas County." Flynn chuckled. "You left farm country for cattle country."

"We like it," she said. She wouldn't move back for anything.

"Any schools around here?" Flynn asked.

"Closest is Jake's Crossing, but it's too far for us to go." Sadie studied him with her head tilted. "You a teacher?"

Flynn hesitated. "I was." But it seemed like in a different lifetime. He was surprised she'd even ask since he wasn't dressed at all like he'd dressed as a teacher. Nor did he talk like one. He'd been eighteen his first year of teaching and that was eight years ago. By the time he was twenty-two and

Rebecca had turned down his marriage proposal for the third time he'd had enough. Teaching didn't pay off. But he'd learned how to deal with people and he'd learned how to use his glib tongue to con good folks out of good money.

Suddenly Sadie pointed ahead at the two sod houses, the sod chicken house they'd just built, and the sod barn. One lone tree stood in front of the larger sod house. It was the only tree on the ranch. Caleb had planted it special for Momma. "There's the Circle Y," Sadie said proudly. Just then she caught sight of Caleb and Riley riding up with Tanner running alongside of Apple. "And there's Daddy and Riley ridin' in. They're gonna be happy to meet you."

Flynn studied the two men on horseback, then looked at Sadie. She was smiling right at him as if he was special. His heart jerked. She was a sweet, hard-working girl. Could he really con these good folks? His jaw tightened. He could and he would!

In the ranch yard Sadie jumped down from the wagon and ran to Caleb as he reined in and dismounted in one easy movement. "Daddy, this is Flynn Greer on the wagon and Barr Eldred on the palomino. Flynn helped me catch Babe! He and Barr are goin' to stay for singin' and Bible readin'!"

Caleb pushed back his wide-brimmed hat and smiled down at Sadie, then looked across to where Flynn was jumping down from the wagon. Caleb walked forward with his hand out. "Glad to meet you." He greeted him in his soft Texas drawl. "It was mighty nice of you to rope Babe for Sadie Rose."

Flynn liked Caleb immediately. He gripped his hand and smiled. "You have a fine daughter, York."

"Thank you." Caleb turned to Barr as he dismounted. "Welcome to our home, Barr. You hungry?"

16

Barr nodded.

"Sadie Rose, take him inside and get him some breakfast. And see that he gets warm. We'll be in as soon as we take care of Babe and the horses." Caleb turned to Flynn. "We'll put the horses in the corral, then get you some breakfast too."

"Thank you," Flynn replied.

Sadie walked beside Barr toward the sod house with the tree in front of it. Baby Joey cried as they walked past the smaller sod house. "Momma's Michigan cousins are stayin' here until they find where they want to live," Sadie said. She didn't tell him they'd already been there several months without making an effort to find another place or a job.

Barr hesitated outside the sod house door. "Maybe your ma won't want me inside."

"Sure she will! She likes company." Sadie opened the door and exclaimed excitedly, "Momma, we got company!"

2
Sunday Meeting

"This is Barr Eldred!" Sadie proclaimed as if he were the most important person in the world.

His heart racing, Barr hesitated in the door-way.

Sadie stepped aside for Barr to walk past her into the warm kitchen. The sod house had two rooms—the kitchen and the bedroom. Web and Helen sat at the long table near the front window. Opal stood near a tall cupboard and Momma worked at the cast-iron kitchen range. Light from the windows and from a kerosene lamp brightened the kitchen. A piece of sheeting was hooked to the ceiling over the stove and another over the table to keep dirt from falling into the food.

Barr took two steps inside and stopped on the hard dirt-packed floor. The warmth wrapped around him and immediately took away his chill. The smells of cooking food made his mouth water.

Her round cheeks flushed red from standing over the stove, Momma turned with a glad smile.

Barr's heart leaped. She didn't look like his tiny ma had. Sadie's ma was short and plump, but her eyes were full of the same love he remembered. An apron covered her brown calico dress. He took a step toward her, suddenly hungry for more than food.

"Barr, come right in," said Momma, taking his thin, dirt-encrusted hand and tugging him forward.

Her touch sent a thrill through him.

"This is Opal." Momma introduced them, still holding Barr's hand.

Opal smiled and said, "Hello."

"And this is Web."

"Howdy," said Web.

"And Helen," Momma continued.

"Hi," said Helen with an impish grin.

Barr barely glanced at the others. He couldn't get enough of looking at Momma. He didn't want her to turn loose of his hand.

"Wash up right there at the wash basin, then sit down and let me get you some pancakes from the warming oven." Momma squeezed his hand and smiled into his eyes.

He wanted to throw his arms around her and have her hold him tight. He wanted to call her Ma and have her call him Son. He wanted that more than he wanted pancakes and a warm fire. Tears burned the backs of his eyes, taking him by surprise.

He'd thought his tears had dried up years ago.

Momma turned to Sadie. "Go change. Opal left water by your bed for you to wash in."

Sadie hurried to her room. The white sheeting was still pulled across to divide the large room into three small bedrooms. She, Opal, and Helen shared a bed. Riley and Web slept together and the third room was for Momma and Caleb.

Sadie pulled off her everyday dress and hung it on the peg stuck deep in the sod wall.

From the kitchen she heard the family talking to Barr. To her surprise he talked to them. Maybe he wasn't as shy as she'd thought. As she slipped on her Sunday dress she heard Caleb, Riley, and Flynn come in. As Caleb introduced him Sadie peeked out quickly to watch Opal. Sadie bit back a giggle. Opal was smitten! She was staring at Flynn as if she'd never seen a handsome man before.

Flynn looked around at the family and thought about walking away without trying to sell them anything. They were nice people. He liked the way Opal looked at him as if he was the only man in the world. The others listened to every word he said as if his words were pure gold. He saw Barr eating as if he wouldn't quit, while Bess York sat beside him and offered him more.

At the table Flynn sat on the bench beside Riley and next to Caleb on his chair. The room was warm and cozy and full of love. "You have a fine family, York," Flynn commented as he buttered the pancakes Helen set before him.

"The best." Caleb smiled at Momma with such love that Sadie blushed.

Opal saw Sadie peeking out, and when Flynn started a discussion with Caleb about the chance of more land being opened under the Homestead Act she slipped into the bedroom. She pulled Sadie over near their bed and whispered, "Is he married?"

"No," Sadie whispered with a little giggle. She

quickly slipped on stockings and her new shoes. For the first time this morning her feet felt warm.

"He's so handsome! And so nice!" Opal said with her hand over her racing heart. Her nutmeg-brown hair flowed over her shoulders and down her back. She thought she was too old to wear braids around company. "I'm glad he's not married. And wasn't it nice of him to take in that orphan boy?"

"Flynn's too old for you, Opal," Sadie said as she quickly rebraided her hair, then tied it with string. She'd wanted to buy ribbons, but cash money was tight and they couldn't splurge on hair ribbons.

Opal sank to the edge of the bed and rubbed her hand over the quilt she'd made. "He can't be thirty yet and that's not too old. Sarah Parsons married a man fifteen years older than her and they're happy."

"He doesn't live around here, Opal. After today you won't see him again."

Opal gasped and her wide blue eyes filled with tears. "I can't bear it! There must be some way to keep him!"

Sadie tugged on her stocking until the wrinkle was out. She wasn't old enough to wear dresses to the floor. "He used to be a teacher."

"A teacher!" Opal jumped up. "That's it! We need a teacher. You heard the grown-ups talking about building a sod school house and hiring a teacher." Opal spun around in the tiny area and her skirts billowed out from her slender ankles. "I'll tell Daddy! And he'll tell the others. They can decide today after the meeting."

Sadie liked the idea of having school. She'd see Mary every day. And if Levi came, she'd see him too. He might think he was too old for school. His pa had taught him to read and write and do sums, but he might want to learn history and geography.

Excitement bubbled inside Opal, making her eyes sparkle and her cheeks turn pink. Smiling, she walked back to the kitchen where it seemed everyone was talking at once. She caught Flynn's eye and she blushed.

Flynn's heart stopped at Opal's fresh, innocent beauty. She was part woman, part child. If he wasn't careful, he'd lose his heart to her. A rule he'd followed from the beginning was never to get personally involved and never, never fall in love. Rebecca had broken his heart too badly to let it happen again. A picture of Rebecca flashed across his mind and he forced it away. This wasn't the time to think of her and the pain she'd caused him. But then, maybe it was. He couldn't let himself turn soft, especially not with winter coming.

As he watched Opal a wonderful idea leaped into his head. He could take Opal with him. With her looks and her innocence she could help him make more sales. She'd work out better than Barr had when he was young. Who could resist a pretty girl's smile? She'd bring him a lot more money than Sadie would've with her racing ability.

Opal stopped behind Caleb's chair, waited until he'd finished speaking, then leaned down and whispered in his ear, "I need to talk to you in private, Daddy."

He smiled as he excused himself and walked outdoors with her. The sun had taken the chill off the morning air. Bossie mooed in the corral. Chickens scratched in the sand near the barn. Caleb cocked a dark brow at Opal. "What is it, darlin'?"

"Daddy, Flynn Greer is a teacher! Sadie told

23

me." Breathlessly Opal told Caleb her idea. "You know Momma would be glad to have a school nearby for us children."

Caleb nodded thoughtfully. "You just might have something. Don't say anything until I talk it over with the others and we have a chance to pray about it and get to know Flynn some. He seems like a fine man, but we don't want to make a mistake."

Inside Opal was leaping for joy, but on the outside she smiled and nodded. "You won't be sorry, Daddy."

Later Sadie looked off across the vast prairie at the rolling hills and the endless blue sky. Was Mary coming today? Because of the weather it had been three weeks since anyone could come to Sunday meeting. Would Mary notice how much she'd grown? She was almost as tall as Opal. Sadie glanced over at Web talking with Helen. They'd grown too. Sadie frowned. Web was still almost as tall as she was. It was very embarrassing to be just a little bigger than her ten-year-old brother. Flynn was talking with Caleb while Opal stood nearby with her heart in her eyes. Momma's cousins still hadn't come out of their house. Sadie couldn't imagine how they could stay cooped up so late in the day.

Just then Helen walked to Sadie and sighed heavily. "I wish a girl my age would come today."

Sadie patted Helen's shoulder. "I'm sorry that there's nobody. Someday maybe we'll have neighbors with a girl your age."

"It's very hard being me," Helen declared with a loud sigh. She pushed her baby fine white hair out of her face. "I reckon I'll just have to keep on playin' with Web and Vard Loggia. But they hate it when I talk about dolls."

Suddenly people were coming from three directions. In the their wagon the Hepfords were playing their instruments and singing. The melody rolled across the prairie and brought a lump to Sadie's throat. Nobody could sing like Judge Loggia and nobody could play like the Hepfords.

Flynn heard the music and drank it in. It had been a long time since he'd heard such playing. The sound could've easily been right from Heaven. His fingers itched to join in with them on his guitar.

Flynn glanced at another group coming. He laughed as he turned to Caleb. "Are my eyes playing tricks on me or is that team a cow and a horse?"

Caleb chuckled as he clamped his wide-brimmed hat on his head. "That's our friend Jewel Comstock. The other horse died and all she had was her cow, so she teamed them up. They've been pullin' her wagon for a few years now and doin' a good job."

As the wagon drew closer, Flynn caught a better look at Jewel. She had a hook nose bigger than he'd ever seen. She wore a man's hat and duster. Two young women sat beside Jewel. They all waved. Flynn glanced around and saw the Yorks all waving, so he did too. "Her daughters?" asked Flynn.

"Mary and Kara. Mary's an orphan girl Jewel took in. Kara is Sven Johnson's mail-order bride. He's on the dark gelding. Carl White's riding the white stallion. They all live over by Cottonwood Creek."

"How about those folks? Pawnees?" asked Flynn, nodding toward another wagon and a rider.

Caleb nodded. "Pawnee man and his sister. She's married to Joshua Cass. His boy Levi is riding the black mare."

Just then Sadie caught sight of Levi Cass and her breath caught in her throat. She wanted to run to meet him, but she knew she didn't dare. She watched Riley run to Levi and they fell into step together as Levi led Netty to the corral.

Zane Hepford stopped his team near the barn and the Hepfords piled out along with Judge Loggia and his son Vard. The big black feather in Zane's hat bobbed as he jumped to the ground. "We made it again!" called Zane in his Missouri accent.

Sadie looked for Mitch, but couldn't find him. Who was playing his fiddle? She looked closer and her eyes almost popped out of her head. It was Mitch! But he was no longer the short boy he'd been three weeks ago. He was tall, as tall as his brother Gabe and just as lean.

Hesitantly Sadie stepped forward. "Mitch?"

"How do, Sadie," Mitch said with a twinkle in his dark eyes.

Sadie gasped. His voice had changed! It had been cracking a long time, but now it was a man's voice! "You look . . . so . . . different!"

Mitch puffed up with pride. "Thank you kindly."

"And your voice!"

"Great, ain't it?" Mitch flushed. "It happened sudden like." He looked toward Jewel's wagon as she stopped in back of the Hepfords'. "Won't Mary be surprised?"

"She sure will." Sadie started toward Mary, but Mitch reached her first. He helped her from the wagon. They walked slowly away from it, laughing and talking together. Mary had forgotten all about Sadie. She bit her lip and turned away. Mary had once hated Mitch, but now she didn't. Life was strange.

"What's wrong, Sadie?" asked Flynn in a gentle voice.

Tears filled her eyes and she quickly blinked them away. She couldn't tell Flynn she'd lost her best friend.

Across the yard Opal watched Flynn and Sadie together and jealousy ripped through her. With a flip of her nutmeg-brown hair she ran to Ellis Hepford. He was twenty and sometimes she thought he loved her, but was too shy to say. She touched his arm and said, "Hello, El. It's good to see you after such a long time!"

He blushed, but smiled. "How do, Opal. You're lookin' real pretty today."

She felt a little better as she walked toward Momma's tree with El. They always stood in the shade of Momma's tree to sing and have Bible reading.

Just then Gerda flew out of the tiny sod house with a loud cry of delight. Her glorious mass of black hair floated out around her head and shoulders. Her yellow dress was a bright splash of color in the sandy yard. "Gabe! Oh, Gabe! You're here!"

Gabe Hepford caught her close and hugged her tight right in front of everyone.

Looking tired, Mart and Essie Tasker, with baby Joey in her arms, walked out of the sod house and over to Caleb.

Flynn looked around at all the people and chuckled softly. He'd fallen into a regular gold mine! He spotted Barr who was standing with Bess York. Barr wouldn't have to be on his own this winter from the looks of all these people. Flynn rubbed his hands down his puffed sleeves, then looped his thumbs in his black belt. He'd fallen into a real gold mine.

Sadie saw Flynn's smile. He seemed pleased, but she wasn't. She sighed heavily. It was going to be a long day.

3
Plans

Her head down, Sadie walked slowly toward the group gathering near Momma's tree. Voices drifted out across the prairie. Jewel's voice boomed out over all the others. A horse whinnied.

"Sadie?"

She spun around to find Mary walking behind her. Mary's copper-brown hair hung in two braids from under her calico bonnet. Her blue and yellow calico dress fit her slender body nicely. Once she'd had only boys' clothes to wear. "Hi," said Sadie in a low voice.

Mary bit her lip and puckered her brow. "Is something wrong, Sadie?" Mary asked in her English accent.

Sadie locked her fingers together in front of her. "I thought you were with Mitch."

Mary's blue eyes glowed as she clasped her

hands to her heart. "Didn't he grow? I was afraid I'd be taller than him all our lives!"

Sadie felt like punching Mitch. "Where is he?"

"With the others." Mary motioned toward the group ready to play for the service. "I told him I wanted to sit with you."

"You did?" asked Sadie eagerly.

Mary nodded. "We are best friends, Sadie York!"

"We are?" Sadie asked hoarsely.

"Of course!"

"I thought you liked Mitch better."

"I do like Mitch, but that's different. You and I are very best friends." Mary hugged Sadie. "I have so much to tell you! And I want to hear all of your news!"

Sadie caught Mary's hand and walked toward the others. It was almost time to begin. They couldn't visit while the meeting was going on, but they could talk afterward while they ate. They sat side by side at the outer edge of the group. Momma, Essie, Lost Sand Cherry, and Jewel sat on chairs, some of the men on benches, and everyone else on the ground.

"Who's the man Opal keeps looking at?" Mary whispered in Sadie's ear.

"Flynn Greer." Sadie told Mary about meeting Flynn and Barr as she watched Flynn tune his guitar to El's and Caleb's.

Mary frowned thoughtfully. "I don't trust them, especially Flynn Greer."

Sadie stiffened. "How come?"

Mary shrugged. "I just don't. Keep your eye on them." Mary had lived by her wits after her parents died by posing as a boy for several months before she'd gone to live with Jewel.

Sadie knew Mary had run across her share of unsavory characters, but she was wrong about Flynn. Sadie started to say so, but Judge Loggia held up his hand and called the meeting to order. His red hair stood out on end and his blue eyes sparkled with happiness. He was a huge mountain man from Missouri who'd come to make his home with the Hepfords in the Nebraska sandhills.

"Let's stand up and sing praises to God!" Judge said in a booming voice. He started the song "Marching to Zion" and everyone joined in.

Sadie lifted her chin and threw back her shoulders and sang at the top of her voice as the music surrounded her and drifted out across the prairie. Zane Hepford played banjo, Gabe the hammered dulcimer, Mitch the fiddle, Vard the mouth organ, and El, Flynn, and Caleb guitars. With the instruments and the voices blending together the sound was so beautiful tears stung Sadie's eyes. The singing went on and on until Sadie felt like she was walking the streets of Heaven.

Barr stood as close to Sadie's momma's chair as he could. He didn't know the songs, but he listened as everyone sang. He'd never heard such music in all of his life. If she liked it, then he did too. And he could tell by the way her face glowed and by the way she sang with all her might that she was enjoying it.

Flynn's heart swelled and tears pricked his eyes as he played and sang. He knew all the words to every song even though it had been years since he'd sung them. He considered the idea of turning back to God and straightening out his life, but he forced the thought aside. He'd get on with his plans. He'd stay on here until he was sure Opal would go with him willingly, then he'd take her, leave Barr, and go on to sell his goods. He could easily get folks to trust him with Opal at his side.

Caleb glanced at Flynn from time to time. Yes, they could trust Flynn Greer. He was sure of it. He'd talked to the men about hiring Flynn as the school teacher and they'd liked the idea. After dinner he'd ask Flynn if he would consider teaching school. With all of them working together, they could easily build a sod school house with a couple of outhouses behind it. They'd build it in a central location so all the families could attend without having to travel too far.

After the singing Caleb read First John chapter three. His voice rang out as he read about God's great love. He looked around the group after he'd read the last verse. "Think of it! If we obey God's commands we live in Him. And He lives in us! How do we know that He lives in us?" Caleb smiled and his eyes were as bright as the blue sky above. "We know it by the Holy Spirit! We are His and He is ours!"

Sadie's heart leaped inside her. She'd accepted Jesus as her Savior when she was five years old. She was determined to obey God's commands no matter what.

Flynn squirmed uneasily. He didn't like to hear the Scriptures. He didn't want to think about his past nor that even today his folks were praying for him. He had plans for his life and he'd follow those plans no matter what.

Joshua Cass stood before the group next. He was a tall, thickset man with dark hair and eyes. He held his wide-brimmed hat in his hands as he bowed his head and led them all in prayer. He thanked God for fine crops and plenty of hay for the winter. He asked for God's leading in all of their lives. Because they were going to eat right after, he asked the blessing on the food. He lifted his head, clamped his hat in place, and said, "See you next Sunday. Enjoy the food."

Sadie jumped up. Momma had told her to fill the drinking water bucket the minute the meeting was over. "Want to help me get fresh water, Mary?"

"Sure." Mary looked for Mitch as she ran to the well with Sadie. He was putting his fiddle away. She knew he'd find her later.

Sadie lowered the bucket on the rope, heard it splash, then brought it back up full of icy well water.

"You need a windmill and pump," Flynn said, grinning down at her.

"We know," Sadie said. "Daddy plans to get one as soon as he can."

"Good. I might be able to help him." Flynn turned to Mary. "You must be Sadie's friend Mary. She told me about you. I'm real pleased to meet you."

Mary smiled and bobbed a curtsy. "I'm pleased to meet you, Mr. Greer."

"Flynn, please," he insisted.

"Do you plan to stay in these parts long?" asked Mary.

Sadie wanted to jab Mary and tell her not to be so suspicious, but she stood at her side and let her talk.

"A while," Flynn said. He knew Mary didn't trust him, but he couldn't figure out what he'd done to make her suspicious. "I do have to find a place to settle in before snow flies."

"We have to get the water to Momma right away," Sadie cut in before Mary could say another word. "Please excuse us, Flynn." Sadie hurried off, splashing a little water on the ground beside her shoe.

"I wanted to talk to him," Mary whispered impatiently as she tried to grip the bucket handle with Sadie.

"There's no need to ask him questions," Sadie snapped.

"But what if he came here to rob us?" Mary asked as they dodged around three men who were deep in conversation. "I don't trust him!"

Sadie stopped short and glared at Mary. "I do!"

Her chin high, Mary stepped back from Sadie. "Won't you even listen to me?"

"No! I know how I feel!"

Mary doubled her fists at her sides. "Then I'll tell Mitch. He'll believe me!" She spun around and stalked away, her skirts whipping around her thin legs.

Sadie pressed her lips tightly together as she carried the bucket to the bench outside the house. Another bucket sat on another bench with the washpan and a towel beside it.

"What's wrong, Sadie Rose?" asked Caleb as he tugged her braid.

"Nothin'," she muttered. She wouldn't embarrass Mary by telling what she'd said about Flynn.

Caleb bent down and kissed Sadie's flushed cheek. "I saw Mary and Mitch together. Don't let the green-eyed monster keep you from being friends with the both of them."

"I won't, Daddy." Sadie politely excused herself to go help Momma carry the food to the table in the yard.

Across the yard Opal stood at the table already heavy with food. She smelled meatloaf, scalloped potatoes, and dill pickles. Everyone had brought something and Opal was trying to put it in order. She peeked through her lashes around at the crowd to see if she could see Flynn. He was talking with Joshua Cass and Zane Hepford.

Just then Gerda plunked down a pan of scalloped potatoes. "I am so angry!" she said.

Opal sighed heavily. Gerda liked her own way and always wanted it no matter what. She was much better since she'd accepted Jesus as her Savior, but she still had a long way to go. "What's wrong?" asked Opal even though she didn't want to.

"Gabe says we can live in the same house as his family!" Gerda's cheeks flushed pink and sparks flew from her blue eyes. She plucked at her yellow dress. "A one-room sod house! I refuse to live in a one-room sod house with the entire family!"

Opal frowned. For once she agreed with Gerda. "You shouldn't have to. Gabe could build a house for you."

"I want a house made of wood and brick just like we had back in Michigan," said Gerda with a pout.

"That would be nice," Opal agreed as she thought of the frame house they'd lived in before they'd moved to the edge of the sandhills. "Living in a sod house is terrible!"

"Bugs and spiders!" Gerda wrinkled her nose. "And crickets!" She lowered her voice. "And mice, Opal. Do you know that?"

Opal nodded. It was an embarrassment, but they couldn't keep the mice out. "Daddy even killed a snake right beside the table with his Bowie knife when we first moved in," she whispered.

A muscle jumped in Gerda's jaw. "I will not

marry Gabe until he has a house for me! And that's final!"

"What's this?" Gabe asked.

Opal groaned.

Gerda turned to Gabe. He was a few inches taller than she was and slight of build. He had short brown hair and eyes as black as coal. "You heard me! I won't live with your family. The house is too small and too crowded." She stepped to Gabe and rested her hand on his chest. "You can build a house just for the two of us, can't you?" She stepped closer and batted her eyes. "Please, Gabriel."

Gabe pulled her close. "Anything you say, Gerda."

Opal sighed. How she longed for someone who loved her enough to say, "Anything you say, Opal." Just then she glanced up to find Flynn looking at her. Her heart stopped, then thundered on. Would Flynn be the man to say that to her?

4

A School Teacher

Sadie stood near the group of men and listened to Flynn tell about the fine windmills, cast-iron stoves, and barbed wire fencing he had for sale. She glanced at Mary to say, "I told you so." But Mary was off with Mitch near the corral.

"I need a windmill," Caleb said as he looked toward his well. "But I don't have enough cash money."

"That's the beauty of this, Caleb," Flynn said, looping his thumbs in the arm holes of his vest. "You can pay a third down, a third in a month, and a third when the windmill arrives. It takes time to ship it out here, so by then you'd have the cash."

"Sounds fine to me," Caleb decided. "I have a few horses I'm breaking and that'll bring in cash. Give me the exact amount and I'll see."

"We need a windmill too," Zane said, his black

37

feather bobbing in his hat. "And Gabe'll need a stove for that bride of his."

"My wife needs a stove," Sven said, blushing. He glanced across the yard to watch Kara sitting with the women. It was still hard for him to grasp that he had a wife and a sod house for them to live in. He'd shared the dugout with Carl the past few years and had forgotten how much more comfortable a house was. Carl still lived in the dugout, but he'd sent for a mail-order bride just last week, after he'd seen how happy they were.

"I might as well order one too," Carl said. The men teased him and laughed, but he wouldn't answer their questions. Getting a mail-order bride was his business.

Flynn forced back his excitement as he quoted the prices to the men. This was too good to be true. He and Barr had gone several weeks without making a sale, now, suddenly a landslide. He looked around for Barr and finally found him standing at the side of the house looking at Bess York. He wouldn't have any trouble convincing Barr to stay behind while he rode off with Opal. Barr was hungry for a momma.

As quickly as he could, Flynn wrote up the orders and handed the men their receipts. "I'll come by your places and collect the money tomorrow," he said, smiling.

Sadie laughed under her breath as she ran to Mary and Mitch at the corral. "Mary, you were wrong about Flynn," Sadie said.

"How can you be so sure?" Mary asked, frowning.

"She's not sure," Mitch said as he tugged on Sadie's braid. "Are you, Sadie York? You just want to be sure."

Sadie scowled and jumped back from Mitch. "I'm sure! He just sold your pa a windmill and Gabe a stove! And he sold mine a windmill. Joshua Cass ordered barbed wire."

Mary folded her arms. "How does that prove anything?"

"Oh, you're too pig-headed!" Sadie cried, stamping her foot.

"So are you!" Mary snapped, pushing her face right up to Sadie's. "You always think you're right even when you're wrong."

"Don't fight, girls," Mitch said, chuckling as he acted like he was pushing them apart.

Sadie's eyes narrowed. "Can't you ever help? You could tell Mary I'm right."

"He can't. He believes me," Mary said smugly. "And we're going to try to prove we're right."

Sadie's stomach knotted. She wouldn't put anything past Mitch. "How?" she asked weakly.

Mary started to say something, but Mitch stopped her.

"We're not telling," Mitch said. "You'd tell on us."

"You bet I would!" Sadie gripped Mary's arm. "Now, what do you plan to do? You tell me or I'll tell Jewel you're suspicious of Flynn. She won't like that at all since she likes him." If Jewel liked a person, she wouldn't let anybody badmouth him.

"Tell her if you want," Mary declared, turning away from Sadie to lean on the top rail of the corral. "Even if she gets mad I'll still feel the same way."

Sadie's temper flared. "Why are you being so stubborn?"

"Why are you?" Mary asked over her shoulder.

"You could help us learn the truth, Sadie,"

Mitch said, as he leaned against the corral beside Mary. Netty ran to him and nuzzled his arm.

"I will never snoop on Flynn!" Sadie walked away, her fists doubled at her sides, her jaw set stubbornly. She stopped on the far side of the sod barn, closed her eyes, and tried to force away her anger.

Levi ran from the barn to Sadie's side. He pushed his wide-brimmed hat to the back of his head. His brown eyes softened as he looked at Sadie. "What's wrong?" he asked. "I heard you and Mary arguing. Are you hurt?"

Sadie plucked at the sides of her skirt. "I'm all right. Did you hear what we said?"

"No. What was it?"

"I can't tell you." She wouldn't tell Levi what she and Mary had fought over or he might tell his paw. Joshua Cass was the only law in the area since they didn't have real lawmen yet. Joshua might feel it was his duty to check up on Flynn.

"Are you sure you're all right?"

"I'm just fine!" Sadie looked past Levi at the barn. "Where's Riley?"

"He's setting up a game of horseshoe. Want to play?"

Sadie shook her head. Normally she would've agreed immediately, especially if Levi asked her, but she had too much on her mind.

Just then Caleb whistled loudly to call everyone together. Sadie ran to the crowd around Caleb and tried to see what was going on. She was too short to see anything. She squirmed through the others until she was up near the front beside Helen and Web. Everyone was talking at once.

"Daddy's got good news," Helen whispered.

Sadie could tell by Caleb's face that he wanted to say something important.

Caleb held up his hand for silence. "Folks, we've been tryin' to get civilization out here in the sandhills for some time. Today we made a giant step." He pulled Flynn to his side. "Flynn Greer has agreed to be our new schoolmaster. He taught several years and is willing to teach for us. We can't pay him a whole lot, but he says it's not important."

"Learning is important," Flynn said.

Sadie clapped and cheered with the others. She wanted to find Mary and say, "I told you so!" She glanced around for Mary, but couldn't see her. She did see Barr. He was staring at Flynn with a surprised look on his face.

When the noise died down Caleb said, "We're going to build a sod school house at the edge of the Circle Y. It won't be too far for anyone to travel. Flynn said he can camp-out in his covered wagon wherever he's welcome. I invited him here first."

Opal's legs trembled. She felt so weak she had to catch El's arm to keep from falling. She'd never heard better news.

"You all right?" El whispered in her ear.

"Just fine," she whispered while her heart sang. Oh, she was more than fine! Her dream was finally coming true! Flynn would fall in love with her and marry her. They'd live happily ever after.

"Maybe you should sit down," he whispered.

"I'm fine. Really," Opal said as she pulled away from El. From now on no man would touch her except Flynn Greer!

Caleb silenced everyone again. "We'll build the school tomorrow," he said. "And start school as soon as we can. We'll have to use the books that we each have. Flynn says he has several in his wagon."

"I'll help build the school even though I never built a sod building before," Flynn volunteered. "And since I'll see all of you men tomorrow, I'll collect your money then. As long as you agree."

They agreed just as Sadie knew they would.

"I'll get the order sent off in the mail as soon as I get to Jake's Crossing." Flynn smiled even though he wanted to leap high and kick his heels. He was going to make more money off this con than any other.

A few minutes later while the other men went to play horseshoe Flynn took Barr aside near their wagon and said, "What do you think?"

"You'll make a right good teacher," he said grimly.

"I am a good teacher!"

"Don't get all riled up. I was only sayin' you would make a good teacher. Just how long do you plan on doin' it?"

"A couple of months, I figure."

Barr grinned. Two months in one place! It was more than he'd counted on.

Just then Flynn heard movement nearby. A chill ran down his spine. He glanced around just as Mary ducked out of sight behind the barn. Had she heard him? He shrugged. What if she had? He could talk his way out of anything. Nobody would believe her over him. Now, Sadie would be a different matter. If he got on the wrong side of her, she'd make sure everyone believed her over him. She'd prove she was right! He knew that as well as he knew his own name. He'd make sure he stayed on her good side. And on Opal's too. His heart jerked strangely. He'd have to guard himself carefully to keep from falling under her power. The love she gave a man would be innocent, pure, and strong.

No woman had ever given him that kind of love. He leaned weakly against his wagon. Maybe he shouldn't fight against taking and giving her love. Didn't every man deserve to be loved completely and to love completely once in his life?

He turned and searched the yard until he found Opal. She was watching him just as she had all day. He smiled, then glanced to her left. El Hepford was watching her. He looked over at Flynn and he scowled, then he stepped close to Opal as if to say she was his.

Flynn turned away. "Well, well," he muttered. "This might not be as easy as I thought."

Across the yard Opal turned on El and smiled. "Did you want something?"

El shrugged. "Would you like to take a walk?"

Opal looked across at Flynn, but his back was to her. "I guess so. But we can't go far." She fell into step beside him.

He started to walk to the far side of the house out into the open prairie, but instead turned her toward the wagons. He wanted Flynn to see Opal was with him.

Opal hesitated, then lifted her head high and walked beside El. At Flynn's wagon she walked right past him, then turned as if she'd just noticed him. "We're goin' for a walk, Flynn. Would you care to join us?"

El stiffened. If Flynn took one step toward them, he'd lay him flat out on the ground.

Flynn saw the fight in El's eyes. Just for the pure fun of it he almost agreed, but instead shook his head. "I want to talk with Joshua Cass before he leaves. We'll walk another time, Opal." He stressed her name just to get under El's skin. It

43

worked. Flynn hid a chuckle as he saw El struggling to control himself.

"Another time, Flynn," she said sweetly.

El's stomach knotted. He walked stiffly away from Flynn's wagon with Opal beside him.

"He's a nice man," Opal said lightly.

"Uh huh," said El grimly. His love for Opal tore at him. He wanted to tell her how he felt, but he couldn't force the words out. In silence he walked beside her into the prairie toward the spot where the bright blue sky rested on a faded green hills.

5
The Sod School

Just before noon Sadie slid off Apple and let the reins hang to the ground. Shielding her eyes from the sun with her hand, Sadie stood beside their wagon and watched as Dick and Jane plodded slowly forward with the plow hooked behind them and Riley walking beside it. The reins hung around his neck and dangled down his broad shoulders as he gripped the plow handles with large hands callused from years of farming and ranching. The plow cut deep into the sod, turning it over in long strips. Birds flew down and pecked at worms and bugs. Wind whirled dust and at times almost tipped the birds.

Her back to the wind, Sadie watched Caleb and Zane cut the sod into oblong chunks that Flynn and Barr carried to El and Gabe. They stacked them on top of each other with the grassy side out and the roots sticking through on the inside. They left places for two windows and one door. It was strange to see a partial building where once there'd been only prairie grass.

Sadie heard Judge Loggia and Cousin Mart talk as they sawed and hammered lumber, creating benches from the material Judge had donated. Mart was telling about working as a carpenter in Michigan.

"I planned on building when I got here. I didn't know there weren't any trees," Mart said. "The whole state of Michigan is covered with trees."

"There's building goin' on at Vida," Judge said. "You could check there for work."

"Vida," Mart replied thoughtfully. "I might do that."

Sadie wondered if he would. He hadn't checked on any job since they'd arrived from Michigan during the summer.

Fighting against the wind, Sadie spread food out in the back of the wagon, then called, "Time to eat!" Momma had sent cornbread, beans, fried chicken, and four apple pies. Sadie's stomach growled with hunger. She'd eaten pancakes and fried eggs just after daylight this morning.

Talking and laughing, the men washed in the water Caleb had carried from home in the wagon. Until they could get a well dug, they'd take turns bringing water each day to the site where the school was being built.

His shirt sleeves rolled almost to his elbows, Flynn washed, stepped away from the wash basin, and flexed his sore muscles. It had been a long time since he'd done this much physical labor, but it felt good. He turned to Barr as he joined him at the

46

basin, water clinging to his shaggy brown hair. "Have you decided about school?"

Barr shrugged, then nodded. Momma had said he should go, so he was going. He called her Mrs. York to her face, but in his mind she was "Momma." He told Flynn, "I'll go. The two months anyway."

Flynn shot a look around to make sure nobody had heard Barr. Nobody had and Flynn breathed easier. "You watch what you say," he warned in a low, tight voice.

Barr pulled his cap on and tugged it down low on his forehead. Someday he wouldn't have to put up with Flynn bossing him around. If he could, he'd stay with the Yorks when it came time for Flynn to leave. But would they have him? They already had a houseful. What was it like to have brothers and sisters? He'd like to find out.

Flynn walked to Sadie and said, "You're just in time. We were getting mighty hungry. I was ready to grab one of those birds flying out there and eat it."

Sadie laughed. She'd almost been late because at the last minute Opal had wanted to come instead. Momma had reminded Opal of the shirt she was sewing for Web. Opal had wanted to argue, but she hadn't. She knew Momma wouldn't allow it.

"I'll ask the blessing on the food," Caleb said, taking off his hat. Wind tousled his brown hair.

Flynn's stomach flip-flopped. Praying people brought back too many memories. Impatiently he pulled off his hat and bowed his head.

Sadie bowed her head while Caleb thanked God for each one helping with the school and for the food.

"And Heavenly Father, thank You for bringin'

Flynn and Barr to us," Caleb said in his Texas drawl. "Bless them abundantly and flood them with Your love. In Jesus' Name, Amen."

"Amen," echoed the others.

Flynn awkwardly clamped his hat back in place. Hearing Caleb pray for him was very unsettling. He knew his folks were praying for him, but it was worse to have someone right here praying too. He wanted to run away as far as he could, but there was too much at stake. He'd have to put up a wall against the prayers and stick it out.

Mart stepped to the back of the wagon first. Sawdust clung to his blue shirt and dark pants. "I don't mind being first in line," he declared as he filled his plate.

Judge clamped his hand on Caleb's shoulder. Judge stood a head and shoulders over Caleb and was twice as broad. "I told your cousin here there was buildin' goin' on at Vida. Once this school is built he might go there and check it out."

"Good idea," Caleb agreed, nodding.

Sadie ducked her head to hide a smile. She knew how badly Caleb wanted to have Mart and Essie move. They were Momma's cousins and he wanted to help them all he could, but his patience was wearing thin.

"I thought of goin' to Vida during Vida Days in August," Flynn said. "But me and Barr had other places to see."

Barr filled his plate without saying a word. He and Flynn had been in hiding during Vida Days, but of course, he couldn't say that.

"Sadie won the sharpshooter contest there," Riley proclaimed proudly. "And she was up against powerful competition."

Flynn looked at Sadie with renewed interest.

She could run like a deer and shoot straight. Maybe he should take her when he left instead of Opal. "What'd you win, Sadie?" he asked.

"A Winchester rifle Model '76," Sadie said. Her face glowed as she looked at Caleb. "I gave it to Daddy."

"It's right there," Caleb said proudly as he pointed to the rifle in the scabbard on Bay's saddle. "It's a fine rifle. One a man can be real proud to own."

"I'd like to see you shoot against Annie Oakley," Flynn said as he moved up in line. His brain spun as he thought of ways to make it happen. What a crowd would gather! If he charged for folks to see the contest, plus took bets, he could line his pockets well.

Barr looked at the rifle enviously. He'd wanted just such a rifle for a long time. He glanced at Sadie with new interest. Maybe she'd teach him to shoot better. He knew how to handle a rifle, but he couldn't hit where he aimed. It had been an embarrassment to him for a long time.

Sadie fixed her plate last from the little that was left and ate with the men. She listened as they talked about the weather, prices of cattle, coming winter, and the new school. The sun grew hotter and Sadie was forced to tie her bonnet in place. The wind flipped her bonnet strings. With a shrill screech a hawk soared across the endless blue sky.

"Fine meal, Sadie Rose," Caleb said.

"Fine meal," agreed the others as they stood and stretched, ready to go back to work.

"Tell Bess thank you," Caleb said.

"I will," Sadie said. She knew Momma would be pleased that Caleb mentioned her.

Several minutes later Sadie packed the dishes

in a woven basket and held them in front of her on Apple. She waved good-bye and rode away, the wind whipping her bonnet and skirts. She saw a coyote slink around a hill just as a hawk swooped down and caught a rabbit in its talons. A tumbleweed rolled across in front of Apple, but she didn't shy away from it. Caleb had trained her not to.

Sadie kept Apple at a walk so she could enjoy the great silence of the sandhills. It felt like she was the only person in the whole world, even though she knew around a hill behind her was the school and around another hill in front of her was the Circle Y. She rode slowly around the hill and into full view of the ranch. On the prairie to the left of the house, Helen and Web with Tanner beside them were gathering cowchips to burn for the winter. Already they'd brought in three wagon loads and piled them next to the barn. Helen's voice drifted toward Sadie, but she couldn't make out what she said.

Opal sat under Momma's tree sewing with Gerda beside her. Opal's dress was a splash of green and Gerda's pink. Sadie giggled. Would Gerda really learn to sew? She had secretly learned to cook so she wouldn't be worthless when she got married. Sadie couldn't imagine a girl who couldn't cook, sew, clean house, do the washing, milk a cow, garden, and can the produce from it. She'd been doing all those things since she was younger than Helen. Even Helen could do most of them. Gerda's folks had really spoiled her. Now she was sorry for it. But they hadn't learned anything; they were spoiling baby Joey just as badly.

"I hope they go to Vida to live," Sadie muttered. Even Momma was getting tired of her Michigan cousins. They had talked of all the family left back in Michigan, but they'd talked themselves out weeks ago.

Sadie stopped Apple beside the corral and carefully slid to the ground, the basket in her hand. She set the basket down and turned to unsaddle Apple.

Her cheeks flushed, Opal raced to Sadie's side. "Did Flynn say anything?" Opal whispered. She didn't want Gerda or Momma to know of her interest in Flynn.

"He didn't say anything about you," Sadie said as she turned Apple into the corral.

"How's the school coming?" Momma shouted from the doorway of the sod house.

"Just fine, Momma," Sadie called .

"Flynn didn't say a word about me?" whispered Opal as she caught ahold of the basket handle to help Sadie carry it.

Gerda ran to Sadie's side. "What're you girls whispering about?" she asked.

"Nothin'," said Opal, giggling as she ducked her head.

"Is it Flynn?" she persisted.

Opal stopped short and Sadie almost dropped the basket.

"Flynn?" asked Opal innocently. "Why would you think that?"

"I saw the way you looked at him," Gerda said.

Opal gasped and clamped her hand over her mouth.

"I'll take the basket by myself," Sadie muttered impatiently. She didn't want to listen to Opal and Gerda whispering and giggling over Flynn.

Opal waited until Sadie walked inside with Momma, then she said, "How did I look at Flynn?"

"With your heart in your eyes," Gerda said, giggling. "You can't fool me, Opal York!"

Opal turned away, her face fiery red. She pressed her hand to her fluttering stomach. Wind whipped her skirts around her slender legs. If Gerda saw her looking at Flynn, had he seen her too? What if he thought she was chasing him just as Gerda had chased every man she'd seen since she'd come to Nebraska? Opal groaned at the horrible thought. Finally she managed to say, "I don't want to talk about Flynn. He's much too old for me."

"He is," said Gerda. "But that never stopped you from making eyes before."

Opal gasped. "I don't make eyes!"

"This is me you're talking to. You're as big a flirt as I was before Gabe convinced me to marry him."

Opal wanted the ground to open up and swallow her. Nobody had flirted more than Gerda had! Opal groaned. Was she really as bad as Gerda had been?

Gerda gently touched Opal's arm. "I'm sorry if I hurt your feelings or embarrassed you."

Opal stared at Gerda in surprise. It still shocked her to have Gerda apologize and be kind. Before she'd accepted Jesus she'd been terrible all the time.

"I'm going to tell you something, Opal," Gerda stated, looking very serious.

Opal walked slowly back and sat under Momma's tree. Her legs wouldn't support her any longer.

Gerda sank to the grass beside Opal. "You're a very pretty girl, Opal."

She was surprised Gerda would think so. "I am?"

"But being pretty isn't enough. You're kind and thoughtful just like your Momma."

"Thank you." Opal wondered what Gerda really wanted to say.

Gerda took a deep breath. "Opal, you're the perfect girl for Ellis."

Opal drew back. "El?"

"Yes. He cares deeply for you. But he's too bashful to say so."

Opal shook her head. Next to Flynn, El was a mere child! She had wondered what it would be like to be El's wife, but that was before Flynn had come into her life.

"Don't hurt El, will you? He's a fine man and he'll make a fine husband."

Opal picked up Web's shirt. "I'd better get back to work. I've wasted too much time already." She'd learned years ago not to waste anything. She refused to think about El a minute longer. She had to get Gerda off the subject. And she knew the only way was to get her to talk about herself and Gabe. "Are you ready for your wedding yet?"

Gerda flipped back her black hair. "I'm not doing another thing to get ready! I won't marry him until we have a house of our own."

Opal gasped. "But what if he doesn't build one?"

"He will," Gerda stated firmly. "He wants to marry me as much as I want to marry him. He'll find a way to build a house."

Opal knew that was true. She held the needle in her fingers and looked off across the prairie. Would anyone ever love her enough to build a house for her? Would Flynn?

6
School

Flynn smiled as he rubbed his hand gently over the oak desk Joshua Cass had donated. It was smaller than the desk he'd had in his other school, but it was more than adequate. The straight-back chair was comfortable as long as he didn't stay seated too long. He looked at the hard-packed dirt floor and the dried roots sticking out of the sod walls. It was not the frame building he'd had before, but it worked. Good One, the Pawnee trader, had supplied the school with a pot-bellied stove. Lengths of stove pipe rose from the top of the stove and went up through the chimney that stuck out of the roof. Flynn had started the fire with cow chips each morning to take the chill off the room. By the time the students arrived it was warm, so he'd let the fire go out.

Pride in the school and in the job he was doing

rose inside him, surprising him. Outdoors the students laughed and shrieked as they played pump-pump-pull-away. He fingered his tie and rubbed a hand down his suit coat. He'd been teaching for a month already. "I'm having a good time," he said softly. It surprised him. He'd planned on teaching just to further the scam, but he'd ended up enjoying it. Even Barr was settling right in. He was learning and he got along well with the others. The pinched, tired look had left his face and he was even filling out some from all the good home cooking they were getting.

Flynn walked slowly to the south window and looked out at the students. Ten were enrolled, but Riley and Levi couldn't always attend because they had to help with the cattle or fixing fences before snow flew. Vard, Web, and Helen were never absent and they were in the lower grades. Mitch, Barr, Sadie, and Mary were in eighth grade. Opal, Levi, and Riley were higher than eighth, but Flynn taught them what he could.

He caught sight of Opal running fast to get away from Mitch who was It. Her face glowed and wind whipped her skirts about her legs. Flynn watched Opal, then frowned. She no longer looked at him with shining eyes nor talked to him in that breathless way. Had she stopped caring for him because he was indeed too old for her? He'd realized he couldn't let that stop him. He had taken it slow and easy with her, talking to her about school or home. If he got too close to her, she acted like a startled doe, ready to flee at the sight of danger. He had only a month left to convince her to go away with him. He would not take her against her will unless he was forced to.

Just then Mitch caught Opal, then veered

away to catch Sadie. She reached base before he could and jumped up and down with glee. Mitch laughed and ran after someone else.

Flynn chuckled. Sadie was hard to catch in a game and hard to catch in class. Her mind was quick, usually miles ahead of everyone. She was the kind of student a teacher only dreamed of having. Could he take her away to a life on the run? She wouldn't run races or shoot in a contest on his demand if he took her against her will. She would constantly be trying to get away. And she'd take Opal with her even if Opal didn't want to go back. That's just what Sadie was like.

With a sigh Flynn turned away from the window. His plans had seemed perfect at first, but the more he got to know these people, the less workable they seemed. Maybe he and Barr should ride away with the money he'd already collected for the stoves, windmills, and wire and forget about Sadie or Opal.

Flynn struck his fist into his palm. "Am I getting soft? I will do what I have to to make it work!"

"Is something wrong, Mr. Greer?"

He spun around to find Opal standing in the doorway. With the sun behind her, outlining her, she looked like a beautiful portrait. "Opal! I didn't hear you come in."

"Am I botherin' you, Mr. Greer?"

"Of course not!" All the students called him Mr. Greer now that he was the teacher. He didn't like it, but it went with the territory. "You're always welcome."

Opal flushed and her heart raced. She wanted to fling her arms around him and tell him how wonderful he was, but she kept her feelings from showing through her eyes or her actions. After her talk with Gerda she'd determined not to act like a flirt nor be called a flirt. "I saw you in the window and you looked lonely. I thought you might like to come out and play."

"Play?" Flynn forced a laugh. Had he looked lonely? Having her be concerned about him touched him deeply. "I'm a little old for those games."

"Daddy still plays them and he's a lot older than you."

"Is that so?" Flynn pulled off his jacket, tie, and collar. "You're right! But I think we should change the game to Red Rover. I haven't played it in a long, long time."

Opal hurried out ahead of Flynn to keep him from seeing her great pleasure. "Mr. Greer said he'd play!" she called.

Sadie jumped up and down and cried, "Yahoo!"

The other students shouted and swarmed around Flynn. He saw the surprised look on Barr's face. Let him be surprised! It'd keep him on his toes.

Flynn laughed as he run out to the designated play area far away from the wooden outhouse built over the hole Riley and Levi had dug. Warm wind rolled tumbleweeds across the grass. A horse nickered in the make-shift rope corral.

"Red Rover is the game!" shouted Flynn, flinging his arms wide. "Choose teams. Mitch and Sadie are captains." He had played the game as a boy, then again when he'd taught school. It made him feel young again to play it with the students.

"I don't think I want to play," Mary said as she walked to the edge of the play area.

Flynn wanted to snap at her, but he smiled and said, "We need you, Mary." Twice today he'd caught Mary looking suspiciously at him. Had she learned something? Somehow he'd have to find a way to win her over.

Sadie started to stick her tongue out at Mary, then remembered Jesus wanted her to be kind even if Mary was imagining things about Flynn that weren't true. She smiled and called, "I choose Mary on my team!"

After recess everyone lined up at the drinking water bucket and took turns drinking from the dipper that hung on the side of the pail. The last one covered the pail with a cloth to keep dirt from falling in it.

Flynn slipped his jacket back on, buttoned his collar in place and retied his tie, then rapped on his desk. "Take your places, please. There's only an hour left of school today and we have a lot to accomplish." He glanced at his planner, then at the students as they sat in their designated spots—big kids in the back row and younger ones in the front row. Maybe someday they'd have real desks, not just benches.

"Vard, you'll have reading. While I'm working with him I want Helen and Web to do their arithmetic for tomorrow and the rest of you write the one-page report on the important person you read about before recess. Barr, please pass out the sheets of paper." Flynn held out blank paper and Barr took it.

Sadie smiled at Barr as she took her sheet. She stroked it, then laid it on her slate. Because they had no desks they used their slates for support. She immediately started to write with the stub of pencil she had. At home the only paper they had was the paper Momma used to write to her family in Michigan. No one else could use it. Sadie glanced out of the corner of her eye at Mitch. He had given her a box of paper in exchange for a kiss from her several weeks ago. She blushed at the terrible memory. She'd never been able to use the paper because of the kiss and had kept it hidden in the bottom of her crate. She'd gladly donated it to the school. Did Mitch recognize it? He didn't seem to. Paper had never been of much importance to him.

At Flynn's desk, Vard was slowly reading from a first reader that Flynn had found packed away in his books.

Vard held the reader close to his face while he tried to sound out a word. Suddenly the reader slipped from his fingers and started to fall to the floor. He yelped and awkwardly caught it. An envelope fluttered from the book and floated to the floor. Vard picked it up and started to look at it.

Flynn snatched the envelope from Vard. "It's nothing," Flynn said, forcing a grin. Without looking at it he slipped it in his suit coat pocket. Just what was in the envelope? He glanced up to see Mary watching him. He managed to smile at her, but she still looked suspicious.

After Vard sat down, Flynn eased the envelope from his pocket and pulled out the papers. His heart fluttered in the old familiar way as he looked at a newspaper photograph of Rebecca. It was the announcement of her engagement to Van Graling of Denver. After refusing to marry him because he was a mere teacher, she'd married Van Graling who was also a teacher! Flynn pushed the clipping and the folded paper back in the envelope. The folded paper was probably one of his lovesick poems he'd written to Rebecca. He would not read it! Angrily he pushed the envelope back in his pocket. Why had he kept any remembrance of Rebecca? Did he mean to carry the pain forever? After school he'd burn the envelope and be done with it!

Sadie raised her hand and said, "I'm finished, Mr. Greer."

Flynn cleared his throat and forced back his painful memories. "Good. All of you bring your papers to me." He walked around his desk and waited.

Sadie, Barr, Mary, and Mitch hurried forward. Suddenly Mary tripped, but caught herself on Flynn.

"Sorry," she apologized, sounding flustered as she patted his arm. She turned away. "I'm so embarrassed!"

"No need to be," Flynn said softly.

Sadie looked at Mary with a puzzled frown on her face. It wasn't like Mary to be clumsy nor to get embarrassed.

"Your paper, Sadie," Flynn reminded her, holding out his hand.

"Oh," she said, flushing. She handed him the paper and turned back to her seat. She looked questioningly at Mary.

"What?" mouthed Mary, looking very innocent.

Sadie shrugged and sat down.

"Opal, is your paper finished?" Flynn asked as he walked toward Opal.

"I'm sorry," she said. "I don't know what to write!" She couldn't understand how Sadie could fill a paper so quickly and without any effort. "May I have more time?"

"Of course. I'll listen to Helen's reading," Flynn said. "Have it finished by then, please."

Opal nodded. She gripped her slate, wishing she could wad up her paper and burn it. She bent over her paper as she struggled with the next sentence. By the time Helen finished reading, Opal had only a half a page written, but she handed it in anyway. "I'm sorry," she whispered to Flynn.

He smiled reassuringly. "Don't be concerned. You'll do better next time."

"I will!" she whispered. "I promise!"

"We'll discuss it later," he said softly. He looked past her at the others. "School's dismissed. See you tomorrow morning at nine."

Sadie slowly walked out into the bright sunshine. She didn't want to leave until Flynn read her paper. She wanted to know how to write it better and she knew he'd tell her.

With Mitch beside her, Mary stood several feet from the school and called, "Sadie, come here quick!"

Frowning, Sadie ran to them. "What're you to up to now?"

Mary turned her back to the school. "I took this from Mr. Greer's pocket when I bumped against him. It's a picture with a write-up about a woman named Rebecca Halstant. And a note Mr. Greer wrote to her."

"Mary!" Sadie cried, looking over her shoulder to make sure Flynn was still inside. "Why did you take that? Give it back this instant!"

"We have to make sure Mr. Greer isn't pullin' anything over on us," Mitch said in his new man's voice.

"We already know he's not," Sadie snapped.

"The note is a love note telling this Rebecca he'll love her forever and if she'll wait for him he'll find a way to make enough money to satisfy her," Mary said. "That sounds bad to me."

"Give me that!" Sadie grabbed for the note, but Mary snatched it back.

"I'm going to get this back to Mr. Greer before he knows it's gone," Mary said. "We memorized the note and the newspaper clipping. It might be important."

Helplessly Sadie shook her head.

"Hide it," Mitch whispered. "Barr's comin'."

Mary tucked the envelope under the corner of her shawl. "Get that look off your face, Sadie!"

Sadie wanted to shake Mary, but she turned to Barr with a smile.

"I told your momma I'd help pick up cow chips after school," Barr said. "We got to hurry so we can get to work. Web and Helen are waiting."

"All right," Sadie said. She turned back to Mary and Mitch. "See you both tomorrow." She tried to send Mary a message with her eyes, but Mary only giggled and walked away with Mitch.

"She don't much like Flynn, does she?" Barr asked as he fell into step beside Sadie.

"You'll have to ask her."

"I saw her pick Flynn's pocket," Barr said in a low voice.

Sadie stopped short. "Are you goin' to tell him?"

Barr thought for a minute. The York family just might be his family before long. He'd have to keep them all happy just in case. "Not if you don't want me to."

Sadie breathed easier. "I don't. Mary said she'd put it back."

"Why'd she take it?"

"That's just Mary!" Sadie ran toward Helen and Web. "We have to hurry!" She didn't want to answer any more of Barr's questions. And she didn't want to think about what Mary would do next to prove she was right about Flynn.

7

Blizzard

Sadie moved restlessly on the bench. She noticed no one else could sit still either. The last recess was over and time was creeping by. Maybe it was because she was hungry. Or maybe it was because the room was so warm even with the door wide open.

Helen raised her hand and waved it wildly.

"Yes, Helen," Flynn said impatiently. He couldn't understand why everyone was fidgeting. He'd already had to stop Web and Vard from fighting over space on the bench.

"I need to use the outhouse," Helen said.

Sadie groaned.

"You just got back," Flynn snapped.

"Helen!" Opal hissed.

Helen hung her head. "I know, but I got to go again."

65

Flynn sighed heavily. "Then go! But don't dawdle."

Helen bobbed up, sending her thin white braids dancing. "I'll be right back!" she said with a giggle.

Sadie glared at Helen to make her sit back down, but she wrinkled her nose and ran out the open door. Sadie pressed her lips tightly together. Momma and Caleb did indeed spoil Helen!

Opal gazed out the window and let her mind drift to her favorite daydream: Flynn carrying her away on the back of his beautiful palomino to the house he'd built for her. The house was a white frame house with a white picket fence around it and two trees in the front yard.

"Opal," Flynn said, interrupting her thoughts. She jumped. "Yes?"

"Time for your oral report on Abraham Lincoln." Flynn leaned back against his desk and waited for Opal to walk to the front of the room.

Opal smoothed down her calico dress as she walked slowly to the front and stood beside Flynn's desk. She didn't have her report ready, but she was too embarrassed to tell him. "Abraham Lincoln," she began.

Suddenly Helen ran into the school and a gust of icy wind followed her. "It's real cold out there," she said with a shiver.

"Don't interrupt!" Flynn snapped. He'd had enough of Helen's pranks.

"It is *really* cold out there," Helen said, her eyes wide as she crossed her arms over her thin chest.

"Close the door if you're so cold!" Flynn said. "Then stand in the corner for ten minutes."

Helen gasped. She couldn't believe he meant for her to stand in the corner just because she said it was cold outside. She looked helplessly at Sadie and Opal, then at Web. None of them were going to help her. With her head down she walked to the corner and stood with her back to the others. She heard Vard snicker and she wanted to pull his red hair out by the roots. She stood on one foot, then the other.

Sadie wanted to tell Helen to stop fidgeting, but she didn't dare. Flynn might send her to another corner. He wasn't as patient as usual.

"Opal, now that your sister is in her proper place, continue your report on Abraham Lincoln," Flynn said through clenched teeth as he stalked to his chair and sat down.

A gust of wind blew the door open and fluttered pages of books. Mitch ran to the door to push it shut. His teeth chattered from the icy wind that suddenly tore around the building. "Mr. Greer, it is cold out there," Mitch said hesitantly. "You better see about it."

Flynn flung back his chair so hard it almost tipped. He strode to the door just as another icy gust of wind whipped through. Chills ran down his back. He stepped outdoors to find the sun was gone and the whole sky was gray. The temperature had dropped alarmingly. He hurried back inside and closed the door. "School is dismissed. It does look bad out there. Run home quickly, all of you."

Sadie jerked on her coat, then made sure Helen's bonnet was tied securely.

"Is it goin' to snow?" asked Opal as she tied her bonnet.

"It might," Flynn said. "So, hurry right home. Barr, you go with them. I'll close up here and be right behind you." Once again they were staying at the Circle Y. They'd stayed a week at a time at the other homes. He herded the students out the door. Anxiously, he looked at the sky again. There was a good chance of snow, but maybe it was a false alarm. He looked at the students. Levi hadn't come today, so Mary was the only one walking alone. "Mary, you watch carefully where you're going," he said. "Don't let the cold wind blow you off course." He knew she walked the same trail morning and night.

"I'll be fine," she said stiffly, suspicious that he'd pick her out of the group to warn. Maybe yesterday he'd noticed when she'd slipped the envelope back into his pocket.

Flynn nodded, said good-bye to all of them, then hurried back inside. He'd put the room in order, get in fuel for tomorrow morning, then ride Kit to the warmth of Caleb's barn.

A few minutes later several yards from the school, Sadie felt something icy hit her cheek. "It's sleetin'!" she shouted to be heard over the wind. Barr, Opal, Web, and Helen were running in a cluster with Sadie. She'd told Web and Helen they couldn't run ahead as usual, but they all had to stay together.

Fearfully Opal looked around, holding the front of her coat up over her mouth and nose to shield them. She stumbled. "Look!" When the others stopped she pointed to what looked like a white wall coming toward them.

"Snow," Sadie whispered, trembling so badly she almost collapsed.

"Let's run fast so we can beat it home!" shouted Web.

"No!" cried Sadie. "We have to run back to the school. It's closer!"

"We have to get home," Barr insisted. "Momma will worry."

"Don't argue!" Sadie shouted as she grabbed Helen's hand. "We have to run to the school as fast as we can. Opal, take Web's hand! Come on, Barr!"

Her head down and gripping Helen's cold hand, Sadie ran into the wind toward the school and toward the wall of white. Would the wall beat them? Would they get caught in the snow and run right past the school to be lost in the prairie? "Help us, Jesus," she prayed as she ran faster. Helen stumbled, but Sadie's firm hold kept her from falling.

Opal's lungs ached from the cold. Her nostrils felt like icicles. She clung to Web as they raced after Sadie and Helen.

Barr trembled as he ran. In the Dakota Territory last winter, he and Flynn had been caught in a blizzard and almost died. They'd found shelter in time. But what would happen in the small sod building? Was it possible to keep warm in it and be safe? Was Bess York safe in her house or was she worrying about them? Barr groaned deep inside. He knew she'd be worrying, but also praying. He noticed how often she prayed. It made him want to pray too, but he didn't know how. Nor did he know God to talk to personally.

With one mighty effort, Sadie reached the door of the school and pushed it open. She shoved Helen inside, then almost fell in behind her. Helen sank to the floor, shivering with fear and cold. Sadie stood beside her and cried, "A blizzard's comin'!"

Flynn's face turned as white as his shirt as he ran to the door just as Opal, Web, and Barr ran in. He looked out and saw the white wall heading toward the school. He started to slam the door shut when Mitch and Vard ran up, blue with cold. They rushed inside, shivering too much to speak.

"What about Mary?" Sadie whispered, her eyes large with fear.

"She'll freeze to death!" cried Opal, wringing her hands. "She only had a shawl to wear!"

"I'll get her," Flynn said as he grabbed his heavy coat and clamped on his hat.

Opal cried out as he opened the door. "Be careful, Flynn!" she said hoarsely. She didn't care if he saw her concern or the love in her eyes.

He smiled at her and nodded, then ran into the wind to saddle Kit. A bedroll was tied behind the saddle. Kit whinnied and bulked at leaving the corral. Flynn hunched down into his jacket and kneed Kit into a gallop. He'd have to get Mary and take her back to the school. She couldn't be far even if she ran. She'd promised Jewel she wouldn't leave the trail in case she got lost. Mary had said she wouldn't get lost, but she'd promised anyway.

Finally Flynn caught sight of Mary running at top speed, her skirts flapping and her shawl tight around her. He knew she was freezing cold. "Mary!" he shouted. The wind tore her name from him and sent it off across the prairie.

She turned and saw him riding down on her. For a minute she thought he planned to run her down, but instead he stopped and lifted her up in front of him. Whimpering, Mary snuggled into Flynn, thankful for any warmth. Fighting against the wind, he unrolled the bedroll and wrapped it around her, then urged Kit back toward the school. Snow swirled around them, then suddenly enveloped them, making Flynn lose all sense of direction. He gave Kit his head. Snow covered Flynn's hat and bit into his cheeks. His hands felt like blocks of ice as he clung to the reins. He bent his head into Mary to keep his nostrils from freezing.

In the school Sadie stood with Opal at the window and watched the snow swirl wildly, blocking out everything but whiteness. Tears burned the backs of Sadie's eyes.

"He won't find Mary," Mitch said, his voice caught in this throat. "He knows she don't like him and he'll let her die out there."

Opal whirled on Mitch. "He'll bring her back! He's a hero!"

"A real hero," Barr muttered grimly as he worked at getting the fire going. Smoke stung his eyes and finally the flames leaped.

Sadie blinked hard to hold back tears. Suddenly it was another blizzard at another time. She was snug in Emma White's house, talking and laughing and drinking hot cocoa while outside a blizzard howled. Pa had thought she was on her way home, so he'd gone after her. Sadie whimpered and pressed her hands to her racing heart. Pa had walked through the blizzard, missed the house and the barn, and kept right on walking. He'd frozen solid and snow had piled high on him.

Opal touched Sadie's arm. "He'll come back, won't he, Sadie?"

Sadie forced her mind back on Flynn. He had to come back! He couldn't die in the blizzard like Pa had! "He'll come back," she said weakly.

Something bumped against the door.

Sadie sprang to open the door, but Mitch beat her to it. Snow swirled in, making the floor white. Flynn stood Mary inside, then led Kit in, almost filling the space between the door and the potbellied stove with the big palomino. Kit nickered and stamped a hoof. Barr took the reins from Flynn and calmed Kit, rubbing snow off his face and mane.

"Mary," Sadie said softly as she pulled off the bedroll and shook snow from it. Snow flew around, hit the hot stove and sputtered.

"Are you all right?" Mitch asked with concern as he rubbed Mary's hands.

Mary nodded, unable to talk.

"We were scared," Helen said, while Web and Vard agreed.

Opal helped Flynn off with his coat. "You did come back," she whispered. "I was so afraid!"

Flynn smiled at her. His face felt like it would break. He shivered and couldn't stop trembling. He'd never experienced anything so frightening, not even last winter in the Dakota Territory.

"I prayed for you," Opal whispered as she wrapped Flynn's coat about him. "I'm happy Jesus answered and brought you back safely."

A muscle jumped in Flynn's jaw. If he'd died out in the blizzard, what then? He couldn't face the answer. He caught Opal's hand and squeezed it. "I'm glad you're safe. I don't know what I'd do if anything had happened to you."

"You don't?" Opal whispered as her heart soared. He did care about her! She hadn't just imagined it!

"The fire's goin' out," Web said as he looked in the fire pot. "We're out of cow chips."

Sadie gasped. She saw panic on the others' faces. They all knew what would happen if the blizzard continued and they had no fire. Silently she prayed for help and protection.

"We can stay warm quite a while with body

72

heat alone," Flynn said, taking charge again. "Kit puts off a lot of heat. We're not going to freeze."

"I never been in a blizzard before," Vard said, pushing his bright red hair back. "My pa ain't been either. I hope he got to the house before the snow came."

Silence settled over the school. Sadie knew each one of them was thinking the same thing.

"I hope Jewel doesn't try to come after me," Mary said weakly as tears filled her eyes.

Sadie knew Jewel might do that very thing. But if Kara, Sven, and Carl were with her, they'd stop her no matter what it took.

"I don't want Daddy to try to come get us!" A sob tore from Helen's throat. "I don't want him to die like Pa did."

Opal pulled Helen close and patted her back.

Mitch jumped up on a bench and flung his arms wide. "I think it's time to sing! We got God helpin' us and we don't need to fear!"

Sadie stood beside Mitch and when he started singing "Onward Christian Soldiers" she joined in. Soon everyone was singing, even Barr. They sang three songs, then sat quietly as if they'd used up all their energy.

Suddenly the wind stopped. The silence seemed deafening. Sadie ran to the window and looked out. The world was covered with snow, but there wasn't any flying through the air. "The blizzard's over!" she cried. She ran to the door and flung it wide. About three inches of snow covered the ground. Drifts of it were piled against the school. Fresh air rushed in. Without the wind it didn't feel as cold. She ran to the side of the school and watched the white wall disappear from sight.

"We'll wait a while and then we'll leave." Flynn didn't want them to leave in case the wind changed and the blizzard returned.

Barr led Kit outdoors and tied the reins to the rope corral. Barr wanted to race across the prairie, snow or not, and make sure Momma was safe. He looked longingly toward the Circle Y. To his surprise he found himself praying for her. He stopped mid-prayer. He had no right to pray. He was worthless, as big a con man as Flynn Greer. Barr leaned his head against Kit's neck and fought to keep back tears.

"Get inside before you freeze," Flynn ordered, holding the door open until everyone hurried in. He closed it with a dull thud and turned slowly to the others. "We came through the blizzard alive. We want to stay alive and healthy."

"When can we leave?" Mary asked, huddling into her shawl.

"In a few minutes," Flynn said. "I'll take you home on Kit."

Mary stared at him in surprise. Why was he being nice to her when he knew she was suspicious of him? Did he plan to take her out in the prairie and murder her?

Sadie paced the room, anxious to get home and touch Caleb to make sure he was alive.

Just then she heard harness jangling and a wagon creaking. "Somebody's comin'!" She raced to the door with the others pressing tight around her. She struggled with the door and finally jerked it open. Cold air rushed in.

"It's El!" cried Mitch.

El stopped the team near the school and leaped from the wagon. Feathery light snow swirled up around him. He wore a heavy sheepskin coat with the collar turned up to meet the brim of his hat. He looked at everyone, but his gaze lingered on Opal. "Are you all right?" he asked huskily.

Opal nodded.

Vard ran to El and caught his gloved hand. "We almost got caught in that big white wall!"

"I'm glad you're safe." El blinked moisture from his eyes. "Load up and I'll take you home."

"I'm taking Mary," Flynn informed him.

Mary shivered, but didn't argue.

"See you tomorrow, Mary," Mitch said over his shoulder as he headed for the wagon.

"Tomorrow," she said.

Sadie called good-bye and Mary waved to her.

"El, how bad did the snow hit?" Mitch asked as they reached the wagon.

"Just missed our place," El said. "I could see the snow like a huge wall not far from us. It passed right over your place, Opal."

"I hope everybody's safe," she whispered weakly.

"They're sure to be." El helped Helen up into the wagon, then he reached for Opal's hand to help her in, but she pulled away and climbed in herself. Pain crossed his face as he helped Sadie in.

Opal waved at Flynn. "Be careful," she called.

"I will be," Flynn said with a slight nod. He swung Mary up in the saddle and climbed up behind her. "I'll be home before dark."

Opal lifted her hand in a wave, then touched her fingers to her lips.

El gripped the reins as he struggled to keep from tearing Flynn limb from limb, then feeding him to the coyotes.

Sadie settled down between Web and Helen.

75

"Daddy will be just fine," she whispered. Her stomach cramped painfully. "He will be. He will."

8

Home Again

The minute El stopped the wagon in the snow-covered yard, Sadie leaped out and raced for the house with Barr right beside her. The yard looked strange covered completely in snow without a footprint to mar it. She heard baby Joey crying as usual as she sped past the small sod house. She wondered if the Taskers even knew that it had snowed.

In the wagon El touched Opal's hand as she started to climb out. "Wait," he requested urgently.

Her heart fluttered at his touch, but she pulled away. With her head down she said, "I have to go in."

"I need to talk to you," he whispered.

"No," she said weakly.

He turned away from her and let her go, then slapped the reins on the team of mules. The wagon lurched and rolled through the snow away from the Circle Y.

Opal bit her lip. Against her will she looked back and watched El until he was out of sight behind a hill.

Sadie stood just inside the house, looking wildly around. The room was warm and smelled like cornbread. "Momma?"

Momma rushed from the bedroom. "Children! Oh, I'm so thankful you're safe!" Momma tried to hug them all at once, then finally hugged them one at a time.

Barr closed his eyes and hugged Momma back. He didn't want her to quit, but wanted to make up for all the years he'd not had a ma to hug him or love him.

"Where's Daddy?" asked Sadie, holding her breath.

Momma bit her lip. "He and Riley haven't . . . come in."

Sadie sank weakly to a bench. "Were they checking the cattle?" she whispered.

Momma nodded.

Helen burst into tears. "I don't want Daddy froze! I want him here with us!"

Momma sat on her chair and pulled Helen onto her lap. "Daddy will be back. He's strong. He and Riley are together. They'll come home soon." She looked over Helen's head to Web. "We need cowchips brought in. Barr, please help Web."

"I will," Barr said, heading for the door.

Sadie covered her face with her hands. She couldn't survive if Daddy froze.

Out in the snow-covered prairie, Flynn felt

Mary stiffen in front of him on Kit. "What's wrong?" he asked.

"Nothing," she whispered. She'd felt him slow Kit and she was sure he was going to kill her and dump her body for the coyotes to devour.

"Look how different the prairie looks covered over with a deep blanket of white!"

Mary glanced around. It looked so different she wondered if she could find the way home. "Are we . . . lost?"

"I thought we were for a while, but I spotted those three hills. I recognized them even with snow on them."

"Yes!" Mary laughed in relief. "You're right!"

Flynn tipped back his head and laughed as if he'd never quit. The pressure had been too great the last hour, but it was gone now and they were safe and unharmed.

Mary turned her head slightly. To her surprise she liked to hear Flynn laugh, especially when it came from deep inside him. He had indeed saved her life and he was indeed taking her home. She felt her suspicions of him fade away.

Flynn wiped the corners of his eyes with his gloved finger. "I haven't felt this good in a long time."

Just then they rounded a hill and Jewel's home, a dugout near the banks of Cottonwood Creek, came into view. Jewel stood in the yard hitching Ernie, her horse, and Annie, her cow, to the wagon. Malachi stood at her side, his great head up and his rope of a tail hanging limp. He spotted Mary and Flynn. He barked once and nudged Jewel. She turned.

"Mary!" Jewel cried in a voice that could've

knocked the snow off the hills all the way to the Circle Y.

Tears filled Mary's eyes as she strained forward to reach Jewel quicker.

Flynn urged Kit into a run and ate up the last few feet of space. Kit slid to a stop just inches from Jewel. Flynn swung Mary down. Before her feet touched the ground Jewel grabbed her in a bear hug that almost smothered her. Malachi licked Mary's hand, then sank at their feet. Jewel smelled like wood smoke and bacon grease.

"You made it, Mary," Jewel said brokenly, touching Mary's copper-brown hair and smooth pink cheek.

"And you're safe," whispered Mary, rubbing a hand down Jewel's arm.

Flynn swung his leg over the saddle horn and dropped to the ground. Before he could take a step Jewel grabbed him and hugged him so hard he thought his ribs would crack. She was almost as tall as he was, but broader and probably even stronger. She kissed him a loud smack on his cheek, then stood back from him, straightened her wide-brimmed hat, and blushed scarlet.

"That's to say thanks for bringin' my girl home." Jewel impatiently brushed tears from her eyes. "Come inside and warm yourself before you head back."

Flynn hesitated, but agreed because he was chilled to the bone.

"I got coffee ready," Jewel said as she opened the door of her dugout. Inside, the smooth dirt walls were whitewashed to lighten the room. A bed with a bright quilt covering it stood in one corner; a table near the door and a cast-iron cookstove took up most of the rest of the space.

Flynn peeled off his coat and soaked in the warmth of the tiny room.

"It was scary, Jewel," Mary said as she hung her shawl on a peg near the door. "I never saw anything like it before."

"I did one other time," Jewel pointed out as she filled cups with coffee. She handed them out, motioned for Flynn to have a seat, then sat in the only other chair. Mary sat on the edge of the bed. Jewel pushed her Bible and reading glasses to the back of the table. "'Twas about ten years ago, I'd say. Came up almost as sudden as this, but it lasted five days. Folks died in that one." She shook her head sadly and clicked her tongue.

Flynn thankfully sipped the hot coffee. He knew he couldn't get a word in edgewise once Jewel started talking. It was as if she'd stored all the words inside her down through the years while she lived alone.

"I was afraid you'd try to go get me." Mary sipped her coffee that was half milk and a heaping spoon of honey.

Jewel nodded as she patted Malachi's great head. "I sure did try, but Malachi here wouldn't let me go. He wouldn't let me set foot out the door. Growled. Nipped my skirt, then hung on until I thought he'd rip it to shreds. I finally gave in and stayed right here. Dogs are smart. This one is the smartest. He knew it wasn't safe out there. But I sure wanted to go."

"Mr. Greer came after me on Kit and took me back to the school," Mary said. Then she backtracked and told about starting home with the wind chilling her to the bone. "I saw the wall of snow and I prayed for help."

"God sure answered," Jewel concluded with a

firm nod. She pushed herself up. "I got somethin' for you, Flynn. It belonged to my man. I want you to have it."

Flynn shook his head. "I don't want pay for helping Mary."

Mary saw he meant it and she realized she liked him. Maybe he had done bad things before he came here, but then so had she. She'd changed and he probably had to. Right then she decided to stop trying to find evidence against him. First chance she got, she'd tell Mitch her decision. She knew he'd go along with it.

Jewel lifted the lid on a trunk at the foot of the bed. "I was gonna give this to Mary's man someday when she marries, but I want you to have it, Flynn." Jewel lifted out a small wooden box and handed it to Flynn. "I won't never forget what you done for me and my Mary, Flynn Greer."

With an unsteady hand Flynn took the box. He didn't want anything from Jewel, but he knew it wouldn't do any good to refuse. She was a stubborn woman.

"Open it," Mary urged softly. She knew what was inside the box. Jewel had showed it to her and talked about it many times. Mary was glad Jewel had given it to Flynn. He deserved even more.

Flynn's eyes pricked with tears. He didn't deserve anything from Jewel or anyone. If she really knew him, she'd snatch back the box and shoot him through the heart.

"Eli got it from his favorite uncle headin' west to Oregon back when he was a boy. He carried it with him until the day he passed on." Jewel awkwardly brushed her hand over her face. "Don't just sit there, man!" she said in her booming voice. "Open the box!"

Flynn slowly pulled off the lid, then gasped as he stared down at a very special Bowie knife. He lifted the heavy knife from the box and turned it to study the intricately carved bone handle. It had been done by a real artist. The butt of the handle was overlaid with gold and had an eagle's head carved in it. "It's a beauty, a real beauty," he said softly.

"I thought you'd appreciate it," Jewel said hoarsely. She turned her head and blinked away tears.

Mary folded her hands over her cup and looked pleased.

Flynn turned the knife over in his hand, then carefully laid it back in the box and pushed the lid in place. "I can't take it."

"Why not?" Jewel asked sharply as she lifted her chin and looked down her hook nose at Flynn.

"It's too special to you and to Mary." Flynn shook his head. "I can't take it." He wanted it, but he wasn't about to take something that important just because he'd done what any man would've done.

"You'll take it all right!" Jewel towered over Flynn and rested her hand on the butt of her .44.

"Take it, Mr. Greer," Mary said softly. "We both want you to have it. It's our way of saying thank you and we appreciate you."

Flynn's throat closed over. It had been a long time since he'd received something he hadn't conned someone out of. He shook his head. "You put it right back in the trunk and give it to Mary's husband when the day comes."

Jewel's eyes flashed. "You too good to take what we want to give you?"

"No, but . . ."

"There's no buts about it! Take the box and hightail it out of here. The folks at the Circle Y will be worryin' about you." Jewel pushed the box into Flynn's hands. "Take it or else!"

Flynn slowly stood. He knew he had to take it. "Thank you," he said hoarsely. He gently touched Jewel's cheek, then kissed her.

Jewel blushed, but look pleased. "You sure know how to thank a person."

"So do you." Flynn smiled as he slipped on his heavy coat and gloves. He held the box to him. "See you in school tomorrow, Mary."

Mary nodded. "Thank you again for saving my life."

He wanted to argue the point, but he nodded and walked outside to Kit.

Momma rubbed the tears off Helen's face and stood her to the floor. "Run and get the eggs, Helen. Sadie, feed and water Babe, then milk Bossie. It's later than we think." Momma slipped an arm around Opal. "Help me with supper. Peel the potatoes. Make plenty of them. We'll all be hungry after such a storm."

Sadie slowly walked out the door. The sky was still light. Mule and wagon wheel tracks marked the otherwise spotless snow. Just then in the distance she spotted two black dots in the world of white. Her heart leaped, but she didn't let herself call out. The dots came closer and turned into riders. Finally she made out Bay and Apple with Caleb and Riley riding them. Sadie raced back into the house. "They're comin', Momma! They're safe!"

Momma sagged weakly against her chair, but she didn't cry. She wasn't one to cry no matter what. "Thank God," she whispered.

A few minutes later Sadie's heart soared as she watched Caleb and Riley dismount near the barn where they all waited.

"Thank God, you're all safe," Caleb said as he gathered Momma close. He held her, then kissed her right on the lips, even though everyone was watching.

Web ran to help Riley unsaddle the horses and put them in the corral. They knew tending the horses came before story telling time.

Caleb hugged each one, even Barr. It startled Barr, but pleased him too. At her turn Sadie clung to Caleb a long time. He felt cold and smelled like leather.

"I want to hear it all," Caleb said as they stepped inside the sod barn for warmth.

Sadie wanted to tell what had happened to them, but Helen started the story with Web and Opal interrupting. Impatiently Sadie listened. It was hard not to tell them to be quiet and let Caleb and Riley tell their story.

"What happened to you?" Momma asked softly as she looked up at Caleb. He had his arm around her as if he'd never let her go.

"That wall of snow scared me bad," Riley said as he hunkered down next to the doorway of the barn. Web squatted beside him, trying to imitate his every move.

"We saw it comin' in time to get ready for it," Caleb said, continuing the story. "We just finished turnin' off the windmill and were thinkin' of headin' back. When we saw it, we knew we couldn't make it, so we burrowed into a haystack and waited it out."

"We're glad it didn't last long." Riley chuckled.

"We didn't want to eat hay and we were both mighty hungry."

"Hungry!" Momma cried. "Supper isn't ready! The fire probably went out! Come on, Opal."

"Don't worry if supper's late," Caleb said, smiling at Momma. "Take your time."

"We don't want to eat without Flynn." Opal looked toward Jewel's homestead.

"Mr. Greer, you mean," Momma said, correcting Opal with a disapproving look.

"Mr. Greer," Opal whispered. In her heart he was Flynn, but she couldn't tell Momma that.

"Just where is Flynn?" asked Caleb, looking around.

Opal told him with Helen's help.

"He's a fine man all right," Caleb said as he reached out and squeezed Barr's thin shoulder. "We're thankful God sent the both of you to us."

Barr's stomach knotted and he wanted to yell out the truth, but he couldn't.

Just after dark Flynn rode into the yard. Soft light glowed from the windows of the sod houses. Laughter drifted across the yard from the Yorks' as he put Kit in the corral and set his saddle in his covered wagon. He tucked the box with the knife from Jewel under the wagon seat. He wasn't a hero and he didn't want anyone to treat him like one.

Tiredly he walked to the house, took a deep breath, and opened the door. Heat rushed out along with the smells of cornbread and fried rabbit.

"Flynn!" the family cried, almost in one voice. They jumped up from the table and gathered around him. Barr stayed at the table.

"We just sat down to eat," Caleb said as he pumped Flynn's hand up and down. "Wash and sit. We want to hear the whole story."

Opal rubbed her hand down Flynn's arm. It took all of her will power to keep from throwing her arms around him. "I'll take your coat," she offered softly.

Flynn shrugged out of his coat and handed it to her. His heart lurched at the glow in her eyes. He smiled and said, "Thanks."

Finally they sat down again and as they ate Flynn told them the uneventful tale of taking Mary home. "Jewel was determined to reward me." Flynn shook his head. "She gave me a knife that once belonged to her husband."

Caleb whistled and shook his head. "I've seen it and heard the story behind it many times. She values that knife above everything Eli left."

"I mean to return it. I tried already, but she refused."

Opal hung on every word Flynn said. It was hard to clean her plate, but she knew she had to. Momma wouldn't allow anyone to waste anything.

"She sure has her pride," Caleb said. "But if she wants you to have it, you'll have to keep it."

Flynn nodded. "If you say so. But I hate to keep it."

Sadie glanced up just in time to see the look of scorn on Barr's face as he listened to Flynn. She carefully set her fork down. Just what did Barr know about Flynn that they didn't know?

9
Gerda's Wedding

Opal stood beside Flynn in the yard and watched Gerda show off the dish towels she'd received as a gift from Momma. The sun shone as warm as a day in summer. The snow from two weeks ago was a thing of the past. Gerda's wedding was Sunday and everyone was looking forward to it.

"Let's take a walk," Flynn suggested softly as he touched Opal's back. "I have something to say to you in private."

Opal's heart almost leaped through her gingham dress. Only twice in the past two weeks had she had time alone with Flynn. And it had been only a short time and they couldn't say anything of importance. She fell into step beside him. Maybe he wanted to kiss her! Shivers ran up and down her spine.

"Opal!" Momma called. "Come help me."

Opal sighed heavily. "I'm sorry," she muttered, her cheeks flaming. Momma treated her like such a baby!

"We'll talk later," Flynn said gently. He'd wanted to tell her he loved her and wanted her to go away with him. Somehow he'd have to find a way. "Go help your momma."

Opal kept the pout off her face as she walked across the yard to Momma near the door of the house. "What is it?"

"Come inside," Momma said, sternly. She led the way and stopped at the doorway of the bedroom. No one was inside.

"What's wrong?" asked Opal in concern. "You're not sick, are you?"

Momma shook her head, then pushed gray strands of hair away from her flushed cheek. "It's about Flynn Greer."

Opal froze. "What about him?" she whispered hoarsely.

"You are much too young for Flynn Greer."

Opal gasped. "Momma!"

"I've seen how you look at him." Momma moistened her lips with the tip of her tongue. "You're pretty enough to turn any man's head, especially a fine man like Flynn Greer."

"What're you tryin' to say, Momma?"

"I want you to stay away from Flynn. You must never go off alone with him."

Opal locked her icy fingers together as an argument rose inside her. She held the words back.

"You can't sit with him after supper or talk to him or stay after school to help him."

Tears burned Opal's eyes. "Yes, Momma."

"He is much too old for you, Opal. You're fifteen

and he's twenty-six. You're not old enough to consider marriage even though he is." Momma rubbed her hand down her apron and cleared her throat. "If you can't say no to him when he asks you to walk with him or talk privately with him, then I'll have to keep you away from school, and Flynn will not be welcome to park his wagon here."

Opal cried out in pain. "Momma!"

"I mean it, Opal."

"Can I tell him what you said?"

"No! I don't want to embarrass us or him. Just stay away from him." Momma awkwardly patted Opal's arm. "That's all I wanted. You can go out again if you want."

"I'd rather stay inside for a while," Opal whispered through the sob caught in her throat.

Momma nodded and walked back outdoors.

Opal ran to her bed, flung herself across it, and sobbed into her pillow. Happy voices from outside floated in around her and she cried harder.

An hour later she walked outdoors, composed, but heartbroken. Gabe rode up on Ears and with a glad cry slid off in front of Gerda. Ears brayed and everyone laughed.

"Your house is finished, darlin'," Gabe announced proudly, swinging Gerda around in his arms.

"It is?" cried Gerda, pushing away from Gabe. She straightened her black hair and tugged her calico dress in place. "Can I see it?"

"It's your weddin' gift," Gabe said, grinning. "You can see it Sunday after the weddin'!"

"I can't wait that long!"

Opal tried to smile along with the others, but she couldn't manage it. She peeked through her lashes, trying to spot Flynn. She couldn't see him.

Had he gone for a walk by himself? Oh, what if he'd guessed what Momma had said!

Sadie saw the anguish on Opal's face. "What's wrong, Opal?" Sadie whispered.

Opal shook her head.

"Are you sorry Gerda's finally movin' away from here?"

"No!" Opal bit her lip. "I can't tell you. Please, don't ask."

Sadie shrugged. She wanted to help, but if Opal didn't want her to, she wouldn't.

Sunday morning Opal helped Gerda dress in the white wedding gown she and Momma had sewn. They were alone in the small sod house. "You look beautiful," Opal said in awe. "You always look beautiful, but today, you're gorgeous!"

"Thank you." Gerda nervously tugged on the cuff to get it over her wrist like she wanted. "I didn't think I'd be scared, but I am."

"I wish I was getting married."

"You will. And I bet you marry Flynn."

Opal gasped, her hand over her mouth.

"Don't act so surprised." Gerda laughed. "I've seen the two of you look at each other. I know love when I see it."

Great tears welled up in Opal's eyes. "I do love him! But Momma won't let me talk to him or spend time with him! It's so unfair!"

Gerda picked up her white hat as she studied Opal thoughtfully. "Your ma loves you a lot and she doesn't want to see you hurt."

"Flynn would never hurt me!"

"I don't believe he would." Gerda stood before the looking glass and carefully set her hat over her mass of black curls. Finally she turned back to

Opal. "I think it's time you used a little trick I learned."

Opal waited, barely breathing.

"Pretend to be interested in someone else. Your ma will relax and stop watching you so close, and that'll give you a chance to spend time with Flynn."

"I'll do it!" cried Opal. She frowned. But she'd be disobeying. It was wrong to disobey. But it was also wrong for Momma to forbid her to talk to or be with Flynn!

"You choose a boy your ma feels is safe," Gerda said with a low laugh.

"I will!"

"Like Ellis Hepford."

"No. No, not El!" Opal's stomach knotted and she shook her head hard.

"Then Levi Cass."

"Yes! Levi. That'll work. I know it!" Opal's cheeks turned red as she thought of it. She'd start today! She smoothed down her Sunday dress and checked in the looking glass to make sure her hair was in order. It hung down on her back and over her shoulders. A narrow blue ribbon that matched her dress held it in place. She looked very grown-up. Flynn was sure to notice.

Outdoors near Momma's tree Sadie watched Gabe talk to the preacher who'd come to perform the ceremony. He was about Flynn's age and had dark hair and eyes. He wore a black suit and held a black hat in his hands. He'd ridden up on a mule late last night. He was the man who'd preached at Vida Days. She couldn't wait to hear him preach today. They were to have the wedding, and wedding feast, send Gabe and Gerda on their way, then have the singing and the preaching.

With a sigh Sadie looked around. Everyone

was there already. The yard was full of laughing, talking people. She wanted to be with Mary, but Mary and Mitch had run off together to talk. Just then Sadie caught a glimpse of Flynn talking to Barr. They both looked worried. Maybe she should try to listen to them. She frowned. She couldn't eavesdrop on Flynn! It wouldn't be right.

Across the yard Flynn was saying, "I don't think the preacher recognized us, Barr. You're bigger and I no longer have a mustache. And I'm dressed in a suit, not a vest and shirt. I called myself Fred Bosley, so I think we're safe."

Barr stabbed his fingers through his hair. Sadie had cut it for him yesterday. It was short and combed nicely, not long and shaggy like it had been when they'd last run across the preacher. "Don't you ever get tired of this, Flynn?"

"Yes. Yes, I sure do."

"Then why don't we just stay here? You can keep on teaching and I can learn to do ranch work. I like it! Web even showed me how to rope."

"There's not enough money in teaching," Flynn retorted gruffly.

"Money's not everything, is it?"

Flynn frowned. "You'd sing a different tune if you were hungry and cold right now."

"But all these folks will take care of us if we stay."

Flynn sighed. "I know, Barr. But what about the money I already took from them?"

"You could send for the windmills and stoves and wire."

"I don't have the connections."

"You could ask around, couldn't you?"

Flynn thought of the money hidden away in the wagon. It was a lot of money to give up. In

94

another week he'd collect more, take Opal and be on his way to bigger and better things. "We can't go back on our plans now, Barr."

"I want to stay," Barr said hoarsely.

"Then stay!"

"You mean if you leave, you'd let me stay?"

"If that's what you want." Flynn didn't tell him he'd had that in mind all along. Nor did he tell Barr how angry everyone would be once he was gone, and that they'd take it out on Barr, maybe even send him to the nearest jail. "It looks like folks are gathering for the wedding. Let's get on over there. Walk tall and the preacher won't suspect a thing."

Barr squared his shoulders, but not because Flynn said to, but because he was going to stay behind after Flynn left. It was the best news he'd ever heard.

Mitch stood to the side of the preacher and played the fiddle to let everyone know the wedding was beginning. Dressed in a black suit with a white shirt and black tie, Gabe walked to his place, watched Bess and Caleb step up to be the attendants, then turned to wait for Gerda and her pa. The wedding was to be short and the reception about an hour.

Sadie stood with all the others and waited for Gerda. Finally Gerda walked from the sod house on Mart's arm. Sadie remembered all the mean things Gerda had ever done to them, then grinned, and shook her head. It was over! Gerda was finally going to be in a home of her own away from the Circle Y! Several people whispered, "Oh, she's so beautiful!" Gerda's face glowed with happiness. Mart looked worried. They walked to Gabe, and Mart handed Gerda over, then stepped back beside Essie.

The preacher smiled at the bride and groom.

"We're gathered together here today in the sight of God and these witnesses to unite in matrimony these two young people."

Opal listened to the words, wishing she and Flynn were standing before the preacher. She peeked around and finally saw him. He was looking at her. Her heart leaped, but she didn't smile or acknowledge him in any way. She stepped closer to Levi.

Sadie noticed and frowned. She stepped closer to Levi's other side. He didn't seem to notice. She pressed her lips tightly together. After the wedding she'd tell Opal to stay away from Levi!

But after the wedding Opal stayed at Levi's side and nothing Sadie said or did made a difference. Levi seemed to enjoy being with Opal. Sadie stalked away and stood beside the house while everyone else ate and talked and congratulated Gabe and Gerda. Finally the two drove away in the Hepford wagon pulled by two mules with ribbons tied to their harness.

"I can't believe Gabe finished a house for her so quickly," said Opal to Levi.

"It's a sod house." Levi pushed his hat back and grinned. "I helped build it."

Opal frowned. "Sod house! She'll never live in it!"

"Gabe's hopin' she will. He said he'll promise to build a frame house as soon as he can." Levi laughed. "She's gettin' just what she deserves."

"Are you still mad at her for fallin' in love with Gabe when you thought she loved you?"

"I guess I am." Levi narrowed his brown eyes. He knew he looked like a man, but inside he felt like a boy, especially around girls.

Opal looked across the yard at Flynn. Would

she hurt Levi as much as Gerda had by playing the game she was playing? She bit her lip. She had to take the chance!

Sadie watched Opal and Levi with growing anger. She couldn't enjoy the preaching or the singing. When it was finally over she caught Opal alone near the chicken house. She gripped her arm and said angrily, "Why can't you leave Levi alone?"

Opal pushed Sadie away and rubbed her arm. "It's none of your business what I do!"

"It is too! You don't even care about Levi. You love Flynn Greer and I know it."

Opal gripped Sadie's arms. "Don't say that! Someone might hear you."

"It's true, isn't it?"

Opal bit her lip and finally nodded.

Sadie breathed a sigh of relief. "Then why are you makin' Levi think you care about him?"

"It was Gerda's idea." Opal hesitated, then told Sadie what Momma had said and what Gerda had suggested. "So I don't have a choice. I have to use Levi."

"No!" Sadie shook her head hard. "I won't let you hurt him! I mean it, Opal."

"Then what can I do?"

Sadie thumped her chest. "I'll help you get alone with Flynn. I'll even help you run off with him if you want."

Opal gasped and all the color drained from her face. "I don't want to *run off* with him. I just want time alone with him."

"I'll help you," Sadie said grimly. Her stomach knotted, but she ignored it. She couldn't let Levi get hurt even if it meant she would help Opal disobey Momma. Jesus wouldn't really care if Opal disobeyed just this once or that she helped her, would he?

Flynn stood near the corral watching Opal and Sadie together. He couldn't understand why Opal was staying away from him and spending time with Levi Cass. He was only a boy!

"Excuse me, sir."

Flynn turned and froze. The preacher stood a couple of feet away, a puzzled look on his face. "Yes?" asked Flynn, keeping his voice light.

"You look familiar to me. Have we met?"

"I don't think so. Maybe in the Dakota Territory?" They'd really met in Norfolk.

"I've preached in the Dakota Territory," said the preacher as he twisted the brim of his hat. "It could've been there. I understand you're the schoolmaster."

Flynn nodded. "I have some fine students. Little Sadie Rose is right at the top. Do you know her?"

"Only by sight. She's a fine shot. I saw her at Vida Days. It's hard to imagine a girl shooting like she does."

"You might know Mary Ferguson. She's bright when she wants to be." Flynn had to keep the preacher from trying to place him.

"I don't know her." The preacher studied Flynn a second longer, excused himself and walked away.

"That was close," said Flynn, sighing in relief.

"Why? Do you know him?" asked Joshua Cass as he stepped forward.

Butterflies fluttered in Flynn's stomach as he shook his head. Just today he'd learned Joshua was the law in the area. "I thought he might start spouting religion to me," Flynn stated.

"You seem to know the Bible more than most

of us," Joshua said as he leaned against the corral fence.

Flynn shrugged. "I know my share."

"How long you been saved?"

Blood pounded in Flynn's ears. "I prayed the sinner's prayer when I was about five," he said lightly. That was the truth. He didn't say he'd turned his back on God when he was about eighteen.

"You got godly parents?"

Flynn nodded. Frantically he tried to think of a way out of the conversation. Just then he saw Zane heading for his mule. "Excuse me, will you. I want to tell Zane so long."

"I'll come with you," Joshua said as he fell into step with Flynn.

Flynn's stomach knotted painfully, but he kept a smile on his face. Was Joshua Cass suspicious of him? Maybe the preacher really had remembered and had reported him. He felt as if he was walking on pins and needles until everyone drove away, ending another Sunday meeting day.

Later as the Yorks talked to their cousins about the wedding, Flynn leaned weakly against his wagon, feeling as limp as a wet dishrag. Was living this way really worth the anguish? He thought of the money and nodded.

10
Flynn and Opal

While the others talked about what they planned to do Saturday, Opal chewed her pancake without tasting it. This afternoon Flynn was going to stop by. Somehow she'd have to find a way to see him alone even if it was only a couple of minutes. Guiltily she glanced at Momma. She was talking to Helen and didn't notice. Opal ducked her head and cut another bite of pancake. Maybe she could convince Momma it was all right for her to have time alone with Flynn. She looked at Momma again and knew the answer.

Just then Mart and Essie walked in without knocking and stood beside Momma's end of the large table. It was the earliest they'd been up since Gerda's wedding a week ago. "We've decided to go to Vida to find work," Mart announced.

Sadie bit back a shout of joy. She noticed the others did too.

Opal pulled out of her daydream and looked at the Michigan cousins in surprise.

Essie bounced Joey on her hip to keep him from crying. "We want to live in a regular house again." She bit her lip. "You aren't upset about that, are you, Bess?"

"Not at all. It's time you had your own place." Momma hugged Essie. "We'll see each other from time to time."

"We might even go back to Michigan," Mart said, stabbing his fingers through his light hair. "If I can't find work in Vida, we might go back."

"Have you told Gerda?" Caleb asked as he slowly stood.

"No." Mart sighed. "We didn't know how. We thought maybe you'd do it, Bess. You're good with things like that."

Momma frowned as she rubbed her hand over her apron. Wood snapped in the stove. "I have never told you no before, but I am going to now."

Sadie's eyes popped wide open. She couldn't believe Momma would say that to her cousins. Sadie wanted to tell Momma to tell them she even wanted them to return all the things they'd borrowed.

"And I'd like you to return the bedding and the dishes you borrowed," said Momma, her cheeks red and her eyes bright. It embarrassed her to say such things, but her family needed the bedding before winter really set in.

Essie lifted her chin. "I suppose we can return your things. But I thought you'd given them to us."

"We didn't," Caleb stated firmly, ending the

discussion. "Now, what can we do to help you on your way?"

Mart cleared his throat. "Could you go with us to Vida and help us get settled in? You know the place and we don't."

Caleb looked at Momma and they both shrugged. "I reckon we can," Caleb said. "You kids can handle things here, can't you?"

"Yes," they all said at once.

"We'll be gone no more than three days," Caleb said. "If you need anything you can talk to Flynn. He'll be staying at Jewel's, but he could come and take care of any problems."

Momma looked at Opal, but Opal kept the excitement she felt off her face. "Zane Hepford will be glad to help too," Momma said quickly.

"Yes, Momma," Opal replied innocently.

"We want to leave as soon as possible," Essie said, changing Joey to her other hip. "We've been packing since the wedding last Sunday."

Sadie saw an impatient look cross Momma's face before she turned away. She knew Momma wondered why they didn't mention their plans.

"We'll stop by Gerda's place before we head for Vida," Caleb said. "You folks can talk to her while we visit with Zane and Judge."

"If that's how it has to be," Mart snapped. He stalked out of the house, then called back to Essie. "We don't have all day."

"We'll be glad to help," Caleb said.

Sadie ducked her head to hide a grin. Caleb would pack single-handedly if need be to get them on their way.

With everyone working together, they put the canvas on Mart's wagon and packed it full of his belongings in a short time. Momma got back her dishes and bedding and gave them to Helen and Web to carry to their house. Once again the little sod house could be the wash house and the place to store cow chips to keep them dry to burn this winter.

A few minutes later Caleb helped Momma into their wagon, then turned to the kids. "I'll ask Zane if Sunday meeting can be at their place tomorrow. He'll send Mitch and El to take the message to the others. If the weather is good, you can walk over. Watch the time so you're home before dark."

"Yes, Daddy," Riley said. He liked being the man of the family.

Opal could barely contain her excitement as she watched Momma and Caleb follow Mart and Essie toward the Hepford place. Blackbirds flew overhead across the bright blue sky. A hawk screeched, then was quiet. Opal laced her fingers together and smiled. Soon Flynn would stop by. At the end of school yesterday he'd whispered to her, "I'll be over tomorrow afternoon. I want to talk to you." Now, she could talk to him without any inter-ruptions! She ignored the sudden flash of guilt. She would talk to Flynn no matter what Momma had said!

Helen ran in and out of the small sod house and shouted, "No more Michigan relatives! Yahoo!"

"Helen!" scolded Sadie, but she couldn't sound stern because she felt the same way.

Opal peeked in the sod house just as an incredible idea popped in her head. She and Flynn could get married and live in it! That way she'd still be with her family, but have Flynn as her husband! Dare she suggest it to him? She laughed under her breath as she slowly walked inside and looked at the dark walls and the one window. The room was so small! But for Flynn she'd sacrifice and live in it.

Later she stood in her bedroom and brushed her hair until it shone. She tied her blue ribbon in place and smoothed down her blue dress. Maybe the others wouldn't notice that she'd changed.

Outdoors Tanner barked his bark to say someone was coming. Opal ran out and waited in the sunlight, her hands to her racing heart. Web and Helen were playing in back of the chicken house. Riley was fixing the corral fence and Sadie was helping him.

"Who's comin'?" Sadie shouted.

Opal flung her arms wide. "Flynn Greer!"

Sadie peeked at Riley. He kept on working. She was sure he didn't know Momma had told Opal to stay away from Flynn or he'd stick like a burr to Opal.

Opal retied her ribbon and smoothed her dress again. She waved to Flynn and he waved back. So did Barr, but she ignored him.

With a rattle of harness, Flynn stopped the wagon near the well. Barr jumped down and ran to help Riley and Sadie.

Her pulse racing, Opal walked toward Flynn. Instead of the suit he wore to school, he was dressed in dark pants, white shirt with wide sleeves and a leather vest. He was so good looking she felt as if she'd faint dead away. "Hello," she said breathlessly as he jumped down. Dust puffed up on his boots.

"Hello, Opal." Smiling, he pulled off his gloves and tossed them up on the wagon seat. "Is your pa home?"

"No."

Flynn saw the suppressed excitement in Opal's eyes. "Your ma?"

"No." Opal laughed breathlessly, then told Flynn where they'd gone. "Would you like a cup of coffee or something?"

"Just a drink of cold well water," he said as he pulled up the bucket and dipped in the dipper. He drank, then hung the dipper back in place.

"How soon before we get our windmill?" she asked.

Flynn stiffened. "Before spring."

"I'm glad!"

"I came to get the next payment from your pa."

"I'm sorry. Since he's not here, you can't. He'll be back Monday. I know he does have it. He got it yesterday when he delivered the horses he broke. He worked hard to get it to you on time."

Flushing with guilt, Flynn looked off in the distance where the blue sky met the dull green hills. How could he take Caleb's money now that he knew the family? Without looking at Opal he asked, "What did you plan to do with the money? Before the windmill, I mean."

"He said he'd buy winter coats for us, but we said we'd do with our old ones. And he saw a stallion he wanted to buy to improve his herd." Opal could barely keep her thoughts on what she was saying. Being near Flynn sent her pulse racing.

Flynn struggled again with his guilt, but finally turned back to Opal. He had to get on with his plans before he softened too much. He took her hands in his. "Opal, I've been trying to talk to you for a long time."

"I know," she said softly. Oh, but she liked the feel of his strong hands!

"We care for each other, don't we?"

106

"Oh, yes!"

"I want to ask you something." He was finding his plan harder to follow than he'd thought. Why was she so innocent?

Opal's eyes softened. "Ask me anything, Flynn."

"I love you," he whispered brokenly. And he did!

The words warmed her heart and curled her toes. "I love you!"

"Would you . . ."

"I *will* marry you!" she cried, throwing her arms around his neck. "I will! And we can live in the little sod house and you can keep teaching school!"

Biting back a sharp exclamation, Flynn held her close while his head spun. He had planned to ask her to go away with him. Marriage hadn't occurred to him. He didn't know what to say or do.

She moved away from him and looked in his face. "I'm sorry. I didn't mean to take the words out of your mouth."

He rubbed a hand over her soft nutmeg-brown hair. How was he going to get out of this one? "You're a sweet girl."

"Thank you. And you're the most wonderful man I've ever met. You're kind and considerate and honest to a fault."

Abruptly he turned away to hide his shame. How could he hurt Opal and her family by taking her away?

"Is something wrong, Flynn?" Opal asked softly, touching his arm.

He forced back his guilt and turned to her. "Not a thing, sweetheart!"

"I've been prayin' for us, Flynn."

Fresh guilt washed over him. "Oh?"

"We want God to bless our marriage. And we want to love each other like Momma and Daddy do."

Flynn's ears rang. What had he gotten himself in to? Did he want to take this innocent little girl and pollute her mind? Did he want to see her change into a hard woman so she'd also turn her back on God? A muscle jumped in Flynn's jaw. Anger and rebellion against Pa had caused him to change. Pa had been to blame. But *he* would be to blame for Opal's destruction. He'd give anything to go back in time and change what had happened to him. He would've taken Pa's criticism so differently. Pa had been right when he'd said, "Flynn, your love for money will destroy you. Put God first in your life and He'll supply your needs."

Flynn forced back a groan as he suddenly realized the truth. Pa wasn't to blame for him turning from God. *He* was to blame! He'd had a choice and he'd chosen the wrong thing. And it would be the same with Opal. He might give her the opportunity to turn away from God, but the decision would be hers.

"Is something wrong, Flynn?" asked Opal worriedly. "You're frightening me."

"I have some thinking to do, Opal." He glanced up just as Sadie peeked around the barn. He scowled and she ducked back. "I'll talk to you tomorrow."

Opal gripped his hand. "I will marry you, Flynn."

He trailed a finger down her cheek. "What if we never have any money?"

"I don't care! We'd have each other."

"And is that enough?"

"Oh, yes!"

He held her close and buried his face in her hair. What was he going to do? He couldn't hurt this precious girl! He'd have to leave without her. He groaned. Was he strong enough to walk away from her love? No! No, he wasn't. So why even fight it? In the last several years he'd taken everything he'd wanted. Why should he stop now? He tipped her face up and looked deep in her eyes. "I'll see you tomorrow."

"Tomorrow," she said breathlessly.

He bent down to kiss her, but something stopped him. He stepped back from her. He could not leave her behind when he left. "Don't tell the others what I said to you."

"I won't. I know you want to talk to Daddy first and ask him if you can marry me."

Flynn couldn't answer. He strode to his wagon. "Barr!" he shouted. "We're leaving."

Opal stood very still and watched until Flynn was out of sight.

Frowning, Sadie dashed to Opal and shook her finger at her. "Did you let him kiss you, Opal York?"

"No! But I wanted him to."

"Shame on you! I take back my promise to help you find time to be alone with him. You're just like Gerda! Kissing every boy around."

Opal flipped back her hair and snapped, "Who needs your help?"

Just then Tanner jumped up from where he'd been sleeping under Momma's tree. He looked toward the Hepfords' place and barked his bark to say someone was coming.

Opal clasped her hand to her heart. "Maybe Flynn decided to come back and stay for a while."

"He better not," Sadie said grimly. "If he does,

I'm staying right with the two of you. I mean it, Opal."

"Don't be so ornery, Sadie!"

"I'm only doin' what Momma would want me to do." Sadie started to say something more, but the words died on her tongue as she saw Gerda walking toward them with a bag in her hands.

Opal took a step forward. "I wonder what she wants?"

Gerda reached the yard and burst into tears. "I'm never going back to Gabe as long as I live! I'm going to stay right here forever!"

Sadie and Opal looked at each other and groaned.

11
The Truth

Flynn drove away from the Hepfords with their money in his pocket. "They would've used the money to get lumber for a real house," he snapped. "Why couldn't they be more suspicious of strangers?"

Barr looked at Flynn in surprise. He was angry because the Hepfords had fallen for the con! "What were the Yorks going to buy with their money?"

Flynn slapped the reins hard on his team of black mares. They stepped forward at a fast clip, swaying the wagon dangerously. Impatiently he pulled them into a slower pace. "Winter coats," he said grimly. "A stallion and winter coats!"

Barr remembered how shabby Bess York's winter coat was and his anger rose. "Then don't take their money! Let 'em buy coats!"

"No! I can't! I worked for that money. I took

time off to teach their school. No, the money is mine." But it really wasn't. It belonged to them. What was happening to him? He was getting soft! It had to be because of all the praying they'd done for him. And Opal was praying for the two of them together! His jaw tightened. He had to do something quick. "We're leaving here right after we get the rest of the money."

Barr's heart dropped to his shoes. "We? You said I could stay behind."

"I changed my mind! You're going when I do."

"No! No, I won't!" Barr shook his head hard. "I will stay behind with the Yorks. I could live in their little sod house now that the Taskers are gone."

Flynn gripped the reins until his knuckles hurt. The little sod house! Where Opal wanted them to live as husband and wife! "You're going with me, Barr, and that's that!"

Barr's blood boiled but he knew not to argue when Flynn was in such a foul mood. Somehow he'd find a way to stay behind when Flynn left. He'd have to be careful. Flynn would be afraid he'd tell the Yorks about the con. Caleb wouldn't send Joshua Cass after Flynn. He'd go himself and he wouldn't quit until he'd caught him.

Flynn's head whirled as he tried to plan the best time to vanish. Just where could he go to get out of Caleb's reach? With Opal going with him there'd be no place on earth far enough away to get away from Caleb York.

Later at Jewel's, Flynn stood with her while Barr put the mares in the corral. "Is there anything we can do for you today to get ready for winter?" he asked.

Jewel rested her hands on her gunbelt and frowned thoughtfully. Malachi thumped his tail on the ground. "Mary's out pickin' up cow chips. That's a job that's never done."

"Then we'll help with that."

Jewel slapped Flynn's back. "You act like a man who has to get everything done today because tomorrow won't come. Tomorrow'll be here. Sit a spell with me and talk. I want to hear about your family. Where'd you grow up? You got good manners, so I know you had a ma who cared about you."

A picture of his ma flashed across his mind, but he quickly blotted it out. "We'll talk about my family another time. I'll get Barr and go help Mary."

"You're always sayin' another time! I'm gettin' mighty tired of hearin' that."

Flynn forced a laugh. "I can't be dawdlin' around when I should be workin'. You know that, Jewel Comstock."

"You're right about that! I got to cut out a steer to butcher. Sven and Carl will be by later to help me."

"I can help you too." He'd done his fair share of butchering down through the years.

"There's nothin' you can't do, is there? I like that in a man." Jewel tugged her hat lower, picked up her bullwhip, and walked toward her saddled horse.

Flynn watched her ride off to the pasture, then he shouted to Barr. Gathering cow chips and buffalo chips wasn't his favorite job, but he'd do anything to keep back the guilt that threatened to overtake him.

At the Circle Y Sadie stood in the yard and frowned impatiently. "Gerda, he's your husband and you have to go back to him."

"No!" Gerda shook her head stubbornly. "First he said he'd build me a frame house and he made one from sod. From sod! I told him I wouldn't live in a sod house once I left here. Now he says he wants me to help butcher hogs. Me! Butcher hogs! I won't do it."

Sadie thought of all the jobs she did that she didn't like to do. Gerda would have to learn to work even when she didn't want to.

Opal frowned at Gerda. If Flynn asked her to butcher hogs, she'd gladly do it. "I'd help him," Opal said.

Gerda drew back. "You would not!"

"I would."

"So would I," Sadie declared firmly.

Gerda paced from one side of the yard to the other. At last she stopped in front of the girls. "I don't want to help butcher!"

"Do it anyway," Opal responded.

Gerda threw up her hands in disgust. "You make me so mad! How can you be so nice all the time? You always do what's right!"

Opal flushed knowingly. She didn't. She'd talked to Flynn after Momma had told her not to. No matter how she looked at it, she'd disobeyed. And that was a sin! She knew the Scripture well: "Children obey your parents in the Lord. For this is right."

"We want to do what Jesus wants us to, and so do you, Gerda," Sadie said. "You gave yourself to Jesus and promised to love and obey Him. That means loving and obeying your husband."

"Oh, I guess I have to go back to Gabe and live in that terrible sod house and butcher those terrible hogs!" Gerda stamped her foot. "I don't know why I should!"

"You do too," Sadie said.

Gerda flipped back her hair. "Oh, all right! But I don't want to walk back. Sadie, take me on Apple."

"Should I, Opal?" Sadie asked.

"Let me do it," Opal said, surprising herself. She did want time alone to think. "Besides, Riley needs you to help him finish the fence."

Sadie shrugged. Opal usually didn't like doing things outside the house.

Several minutes later Opal rode Apple across the prairie with Gerda on behind, holding on tightly around her waist. Opal's head spun with wondering what she was going to do. She'd have to tell Momma the truth. But was she ready for that? Was she ready to obey no matter what? She bit back a groan. If Momma said she couldn't marry Flynn, what would she do?

At the Hepfords' Gerda slipped off Apple, grunted a low good-bye and thank you, and slowly walked toward her sod house. It stood several yards from the other house and the barn, and in the opposite direction from the pig pen. Pigs squealed and rooted in the muddy pen. The place seemed deserted.

Opal glanced around for a glimpse of El, then frowned. Why did she suddenly want to see El?

Then, there he was, striding from the sod barn right toward her. He wore faded overalls, a blue plaid shirt, and a wide-brimmed gray hat over his black hair. She wanted to turn Apple and ride away, but she couldn't move.

"How do, Opal," El said softly as he reached up to help her dismount.

"I can't stay," she objected weakly.

"Please." He circled her small waist with his

hands and lifted her down. He kept his hands at her waist as he devoured her with his eyes.

She trembled and tried to push him away. She felt the wild beat of his heart under her palms, and it left her too weak to push away. He lowered his head and touched his lips to hers. A shock went through her, but still she couldn't pull away. The kiss went on and on. To her horror she found herself kissing him back, and liking it!

At last he lifted his head and smiled into her eyes. "Next year when you're sixteen, will you be my wife?"

She gasped. "Your wife?" she whispered.

"You're the air I breathe, Opal York. The sunshine that warms me. You're the only woman for me."

She touched his cheek in wonder. Was this shy Ellis Hepford saying such words to her?

El caught her hands in his hard callused hands. "I need you. I need your love."

She bowed her head and moaned. Was this why she'd wanted to bring Gerda home?

He lifted her hand to his lips and kissed her fingers. "I dreamed you'd ride into the yard so I could see you and touch you."

"I . . . I brought Gerda home."

"You could've sent Sadie."

Opal bit her lip.

"I thank God you came." El smiled. "I want you to stay, but I know you have to get back. But I'll see you tomorrow at Sunday meeting."

She nodded.

"I have to help Pa and the boys butcher hogs."

"I'd help if I could stay," she whispered.

"I know you would." El ran a finger lightly over

her lips. "You'd do anything for your man. Your momma raised you that way."

Opal nodded. She knew it was true.

El's face hardened. "I will never let Flynn Greer take you from me."

She cried out and leaped away from him. How could she have forgotten about Flynn? She had promised to marry him! He was her hero, her knight in shining armor! But El was flesh and blood. He was real. Was it possible that her love for Flynn was a dream and what she felt for Ellis Hepford was true love?

El caught her hands again and held them tightly. "Don't let him turn your head with his good looks and worldly ways."

Is that what she'd let happen?

He helped her mount, squeezed her hand, kissed the back of it, then whispered, "I love you."

Tears filled her eyes. "Good-bye." She nudged Apple and slowly rode away. Before she rounded the first hill she looked back. El was still standing there. She lifted her hand and so did he.

Several minutes later before the Circle Y was in sight she reined in Apple, then sat very still with her eyes closed and her hands over the saddle horn. Tears slipped from under her lashes and rolled down her cheeks. "Heavenly Father, I need Your help. Forgive me for disobeying Momma. I am in so much trouble and I don't know what to do. Can You help me?"

In Vida, Caleb stood in the general store talking with Brother Zack, the preacher who'd been to his house last Sunday. Bess was looking through the store with Essie. The smell of coal oil, leather, and licorice were strong around him.

"I finally remembered where I saw that man Flynn Greer," said Brother Zack as he pushed his hat back. "In Norfolk. But he called himself . . . Bosley, I think it was. And he was a salesman, not a teacher. Sold windmills and such."

Caleb frowned. "Why would Flynn call himself Bosley?"

"To hide, I suspect. He's a con man. He takes the money for the windmills and stoves and things, never orders them, and leaves town a little richer."

Caleb's stomach knotted. "I hate to think Flynn did such a thing."

"I know it was him. But the boy does look different."

"Maybe you're mistaken."

"I could be. But there's a good chance I'm not. You'll know soon enough, I guess. If he starts selling you windmills, be on guard."

"I will," Caleb said grimly. He excused himself and strode to Bess. "I changed my mind about stayin' the night. I want to get home."

Bess frowned. "Is something wrong?"

"Nothin' I can't handle. Tell your cousins good-bye and we'll be on our way."

"Whatever you say, Caleb."

He strode to the door and looked unseeingly out at his wagon near the hitchrail. Had Flynn taken them in? It didn't seem likely, but it was safer to check into it before another day ended.

12
Solutions

Her face set and her shoulders square, Opal determinedly urged Apple toward Jewel Comstock's place. "I must see Flynn," Opal muttered to herself. She had to tell him the truth about her feelings toward him and toward El. After praying and searching her heart she knew what she felt for Flynn wasn't the love like Momma had for Caleb. It was a fairy tale love that had nothing to do with day-to-day living. Just knowing that made her suddenly feel very mature. She bit her lip and sighed heavily. But she had promised to marry Flynn, and because she'd promised, she'd keep her word. She was a woman of her word!

Several minutes later she spotted Flynn in the middle of the prairie, gathering buffalo chips in a basket to put in the wagon Mary had parked in the middle of the area still covered with dried manure.

Mary and Barr were working off in another direction.

Flynn saw Opal coming and he tensed. Was something wrong at the Circle Y? He dropped his basket and hurried toward her. "Opal, what's wrong?" he called.

She nudged Apple forward. When she reached Flynn she dropped to the ground and let the reins fall forward. Her cheeks were red and her hair was mussed from the wind. She pushed it back behind her ears and bit her lip.

"What is it?" Flynn could see something different in her, but couldn't put his finger on it. "Is something wrong?"

"Yes," she whispered. She took a deep breath and looked into his dear face. "Flynn, I have wronged you."

"What? Why?" He was at a loss. What could this innocent child do to wrong him?

She took one of his hands with both of hers. The late afternoon sun blazed down on them and the constant Nebraska wind blew against them. "I don't want to hurt you. You know that, don't you?"

"Opal, please, tell me what's wrong!" He suddenly felt weak all over. She couldn't have learned the truth about him, so what could it be?

Opal cleared her throat. "After you left our place, Gerda came over ready to leave Gabe."

"Yes?"

"Sadie and I talked her out of it. And I took her home on Apple."

"That's good."

Apple nickered and bobbed her head.

Opal gripped Flynn's hand tighter. "And while I was there I saw . . . El."

Flynn stiffened. "And?"

Giant tears welled up in Opal's eyes. "I did something awful!"

"You, Opal?"

"I let him . . . kiss me."

Flynn frowned.

"And I let him speak to me of . . . love . . . and . . . marriage."

Flynn saw the anguish in Opal's wide blue eyes. What was she getting at?

"Flynn, you are a wonderful man and I look on you as a hero."

He shook his head as a tiny shiver ran down his spine. Just what was coming?

"I realized that . . . that I truly love El." Opal's voice faded away.

A muscle jumped in Flynn's jaw. Now he knew what she was going to say! She wanted to reject him just as Rebecca had so many times in the past. "And what of us?" Flynn asked gruffly.

"I am so sorry!" Opal sniffed and bit her lip. "It's not fair to you, I know. I promised to marry you, and I will keep my promise. But I felt you should know the truth about me first."

Flynn stared at her in shock. She loved El, but would marry him because she gave her word! What kind of girl was she? He knew. She was a Christian. Her word was her bond just as his used to be.

"I know I've hurt you, Flynn, and I'm sorry!" A tear slipped down her cheek and splashed on his hand. "You're a wonderful man and will make a wonderful husband."

If only she knew! Flynn pulled away from her and stabbed his fingers through his hair.

"I'll do anything for you, Flynn! Anything!"

Suddenly he saw his chance. He'd take her away now and forget about getting the last of

Caleb's money. He and Opal could ride to Kansas, maybe stay in Kansas City for the winter. They could live off the money he had stashed away in his wagon. He caught her hands. "Then go with me now. Right now. We can head for Kansas City."

She trembled. "But what about my family?"

"You can leave a letter for them with Jewel."

"What about the school?"

He shrugged.

"What about . . . getting married?"

He hesitated. "We'll get married when we get there."

"I asked God to help you make the right decision and he has. I'll do what you say." Opal bowed her head as tears ran down her cheeks.

Flynn's heart turned over as he saw her anguish. He pulled her close and patted her back to soothe her. Love for her rose in him until he thought he'd burst with it. As she sobbed against him, tears filled his eyes. He had never met a family like the Yorks. They didn't just talk Christianity, but they lived it. The cold wall he'd built around his heart suddenly crumbled. He pushed his face into Opal's hair and let his tears fall. Silently he asked God to forgive him for hardening his heart and for all the sins he'd committed. He remembered the Scripture 1 John 1:9—"If we confess our sins, he is faithful and just to forgive us our sins, and to cleanse us from all unrighteousness." He was forgiven! His heart was pure once again!

Finally he held Opal from him, dried his eyes, then hers. He was about to do the hardest thing he'd ever done in his life. "Opal, my dear sweet girl, I want you to stay home with your family. And when you're sixteen, you marry Ellis Hepford and live happily ever after."

Opal's eyes widened and she gasped. "Do you mean it?"

"Every word."

Her chin quivered and she sniffed. "Thank you. I know God will send the perfect woman to you as a wife."

Flynn nodded. "I believe so too." The pain Rebecca had caused him was gone! At long last he was free. "You head on back home now. I'll see you tomorrow at Sunday meeting."

"Tomorrow," she whispered. Now she had another impossible task—to tell Momma she'd disobeyed and was sorry. But God was with her and would give her strength.

Flynn helped her mount Apple and watched as she rode away. He brushed fresh tears away. Now he had some planning to do.

Later he sat at the table with Jewel, the box with Eli's bowie knife between them. Barr and Mary were doing chores. "Let me explain, Jewel," Flynn started softly. "You'll want it back once you hear."

"No, I won't," she said, stubbornly shaking her head.

His nerves tightened. This was going to be hard. Taking a deep breath, he told Jewel everything about himself and Barr. He ended with what had happened on the prairie with Opal. "So, I'm returning the knife and the money, then I'm leaving."

Jewel slammed her fist on the table. The box, lamp, Bible, and her reading glasses bounced. "You'll do no such thing! You're gonna take that money and you're gonna order them things you have receipts for. And you're gonna do it right away."

Flynn helplessly shook his head.

"And you're gonna stay right here and teach our school! That you can plan on!"

"What about . . . what I've . . . done?"

Jewel leaned toward him with a scowl. "You think you're the only one done wrong around these parts? What counts is being forgiven by Jesus and makin' your life count for somethin' good. That's what counts!"

"How do you know the others will agree?"

Jewel patted the butt of her .44. "They'll listen to me and then they'll agree."

Suddenly the door burst open and Caleb stood there with a determined look. Bess stood behind him, looking startled. "I want a word with you, Flynn! I just been talkin' to that preacher Brother Zack."

"It's all been settled," Jewel said, laughing. "Get down off your high horse, Caleb York, and listen to the man." She shoved the box with Eli's knife toward Flynn. "As for you, mister, you're takin' this and you're keepin' it!"

Flynn's throat closed over as he reached for the box.

The next morning at the Hepfords', Sadie felt the tension in Flynn as she stood beside him while the men gathered by themselves on the far side of the yard. She glanced up at Flynn, opened her mouth to question him, then snapped it closed. Something was going on that she didn't know about.

Flynn knew Caleb was telling Zane, Judge, and Joshua the truth about him. Together they'd decide if he would go to jail or could stay as the teacher. If he did stay, they'd agreed to keep his past a secret. He knew he wanted to stay as much as Barr did.

Barr trembled. Flynn had told him what had happened. He knew both their lives were at stake. Silently he asked the Lord to help him. He stopped mid-sentence. Before the day was out he'd ask Momma how he could accept Jesus as his Savior and he'd learn to pray no matter what the decision was.

Finally the men joined the others. Caleb stood before the group. He nodded to Flynn, smiled, then said, "It's time to start our meetin'. Let's pray. Flynn, would you like to lead us?"

"Amen!" Jewel shouted in a voice that almost knocked the roof off the sod house behind them.

Flynn's heart soared. They'd agreed to let him stay! He smiled at Barr, then bowed his head.

Barr wanted to leap high, but he stood still and bowed his head. Tears slipped down his cheeks, and he let them fall.

Sadie felt the excitement in the air. It was a different kind of excitement and she couldn't understand it.

"Heavenly Father," Flynn started. H̶ up and couldn't continue for a while, "Thank You for showing Your love to us. Bless us this day and make us a blessing to others."

Opal reached for El's hand and they stood together with their heads bowed as Flynn prayed.

Sadie peeked at Levi just as he peeked at her. They smiled and quickly bowed their heads.

Later Judge Loggia started the singing with a song of victory. Sadie looked around as the musicians played like they'd never played before and everyone sang with a new joy. Something was in the air, but what? Shivers ran up and down her spine and she laughed aloud. She didn't care what it was. It was good! She tipped back her head and sang with all her heart. The music drifted out across the endless prairie. She wanted it to keep going until it touched others as much as it touched her.